USA TODAY BESTSELLING AUTHORS

J.L. BECK &
C. HALLMAN

Copyright © 2021 by Bleeding Heart Press

Cover Design by C. Hallman

Bleeding Heart Covers

All rights reserved.

No part of this book may be reproduced in any form or by any electronic or mechanical means, including information storage and retrieval systems, without written permission from the author, except for the use of brief quotations in a book review.

ARE YOU READY TO PLAY?

I've built this club from the ground up. A playground for the wicked. In my club, your wildest dreams can come true, or your worst nightmares can swallow you whole.

1

owan

What am I doing here?

I've lost track of the number of times I've asked myself that question. Why am I doing this? What am I doing here? How can I get out of this? It's like my whole life has turned into one long, endless nightmare. And I can't find a way to wake up.

Which is why I'm walking up to the back doors of Purgatory. In the daylight, the building looks like a plain, boring structure just outside the downtown area. It doesn't stand out from the other buildings up and down the block—except for the large neon sign above the front door. Driving by, nobody would ever guess what really goes on inside these walls.

There's not as much foot traffic around here. I guess that changes later when the main crowd arrives. Most people think this is nothing more than a dance club. Few are aware that this is an upscale sex club... one I sent my best friend, Eve, to just a few months ago. Her visit ended with a happily ever after, but I already know mine won't.

"You came," Alexei says. He's my connection, the guy who only wanted to help me out of a bad spot the night he found me weeping outside the diner where I used to work. Mr. Good Guy, Mr. Helpful, Mr. *Let me see what I can do to get you out of this jam.*

I'm not a stupid person, and I've learned a lot in my twenty years.

The thing is, when you've just lost your job and have no idea how you're going to pay the rent you're already two months late on, you might forget everything you thought you knew. That's another lesson I've learned the hard way.

"I didn't think I had much of a choice." It takes all of my courage to stand upright, shoulders back, chin held high. This might be the most humiliating experience of my life, but I don't have to cower and tremble.

Alexei's beady, deep-set eyes crawl over my body. He must like what he sees because one corner of his mouth quirks upward in a smile that gives away everything on his filthy mind. "You don't have a choice. I'm just glad you didn't make me chase you down or anything like that."

That makes two of us. I resist the impulse to cover my cleavage with my hands when his eyes land there and stay there. My mouth is suddenly so dry. I nod toward the windowless door. "Well? Are we going in?"

He draws his bottom lip under his teeth for just a second before my question sinks in. "Oh, yeah. He'll be waiting for you."

I've never been so scared in my life. And that's saying something.

Alexei opens the door and stands to the side, gesturing for me to go in. One glance tells me nothing about what's in there since everything is so dark. I have half a mind to ask for a flashlight, especially in these ridiculous heels I'm wearing. It would just be my luck to end up spraining my ankle or worse. But that was what I was instructed to wear: something short, tight, low-cut. Platform heels, preferably strappy so my feet would be visible.

Because, of course, before I can pay off my debt, the boss has to give the final word on whether or not I'm worthy. Whether he thinks I'll earn for him.

I'm clearly not moving fast enough because Alexei practically shoves me into what looks like a high-end lounge with leather couches and chairs, and a bar that stretches across one wall. The lighting is low and tasteful, except for the cages.

Yes. Girls are dancing in cages. I quickly count eight of them as Alexei ushers me through the bar, spotlights shining on them as they bump and grind in various states of undress to entertain guests who are mingling with their drinks.

There's no time for me to take it all in before he hurries me into a narrow stairwell. "Up."

One night. This is just for one night. That's what I tell myself with every step I climb. This is the only time I ever have to come here. And once the night is over, I'll be free.

It's surprisingly quiet for a sex club. I expected to at least hear some moaning, maybe a few squeals. It was like this the first time I was here as well. The walls must be soundproofed.

Alexei takes the lead once we reach the landing, guiding me down a narrow hall to a door at the end. After three sharp knocks, the door opens slowly by itself.

The room on the other side is not what I expected, but then, none of this has been. It's well lit, sleek, and almost welcoming. At least, until I set eyes on the man sitting behind the desk directly opposite the door, his finger pressed against a button mounted in front of him.

Icy-blue eyes. They almost jump out at me from under dark, heavy brows. He leans back in his chair, fingers tented under his chin, and there's a glass of what looks like whiskey next to the button he used to open the door. Nobody has to tell me he's the boss. Everything about him screams mastery, control.

He nods once, and Alexei takes this as a sign to get me in the room and close the door. He pushes me forward, and I hear the definitive click of the door being shut, leaving me alone with the man who I know is named Lucian, the owner of Purgatory.

That's all I know about him, though, and the fact I owe him ten grand. Although I do know he has a lot of other shady, underground businesses only hinted at online.

What a shame I didn't have the time to look further into his businesses before I agreed to let Alexei lend me the money I needed. Money I couldn't possibly pay back.

Lucian's eyes roam over me the way Alexei's did, but there's a different sort of look in them. Alexei was imagining what he would do to me. Lucian looks at me like I'm a prize cow or something, like he's assessing me for sale. "Turn. Let me see the back."

So much for an introduction. There's nothing in his deep but cold voice that gives me any sense of comfort as I turn halfway so he can get a look at my ass. All I can do is stare at the wall and will my knees to stop shaking.

"You'll do. Turn." I do as I'm told, glad I passed muster yet at the same time afraid of what that means. I can't imagine what I'll have to do to satisfy my debt, but ten grand is a lot of money, and something tells me he's going to make me work for it.

He picks up his glass, swirling the liquor around, studying me. "Your name is Rowan, right?"

"Yes."

"And you're twenty years old?" I nod my head as he lifts the tumbler to his lips, watching me the entire time he does it. I'm afraid that if I don't watch him with the same intensity, he may take me as weak. "You don't say much, do you?"

"I don't know what to say."

This seems to please him. He lowers the tumbler, nodding. "That's good. I can't stand people who ask too many questions. Do you know anything about this club?

"I know enough." Thanks to my ex, who brought me here for a threesome, and to my best friend, Eve, who had a pleasant encounter here with her stepbrother. "I've been upstairs before," I admit, "and so have my friends. But I don't know much about what's going on downstairs."

"We keep it that way for a reason." He folds his hands over his flat stomach, and I catch sight of a flashy watch peeking out from under his shirt cuff. I could probably pawn that watch and pay off my debt with money to spare. "Welcome to Purgatory. This is an exclusive club. We're very careful with our clientele. The fact that you're considered worthy of working here for the night speaks highly of you."

Am I supposed to be flattered? I'm not sure, though a part of me is glad I met with his approval.

"We are discreet, of course," he continues. "Nothing that goes on within these walls goes beyond these walls. You understand that?"

"I do."

"Good." He suddenly stands, crossing the room with long, slow strides and stopping in front of a bar cart loaded with bottles, tumblers, and an ice bucket. Since he already has a drink of his own, I guess this one's for me.

"You're on the second floor currently, and this is the level we refer to as Heaven. There are rooms set up throughout the floor where clients can engage in whatever kink they enjoy. We have strict rules when it comes to consent and a zero-tolerance policy for guests—men or women—who can't take no for an answer."

He turns his head slightly, catching me out of the corner of his eye. "Tonight, you'll be working in Hell. That's what we call the basement level. The main level, where you walked in, is more of a social area. That's where our guests relax and enjoy a few drinks before going either upstairs or down."

I'm afraid to ask but do so anyway. "And what happens in Hell?"

He stops, holding an ice cube in a pair of tongs, the ice hovering over the glass for one little moment before he drops it with a *clink*. "Hell is reserved for our most formidable guests."

That's not exactly an answer, though something tells me I shouldn't press him for more information. He did say he doesn't like it when people ask questions, right?

"You're not thinking about backing out now, are you?" He turns to me, and I can't help but notice his trim body—tall, broad-shouldered, slim-hipped. He's wearing a white dress shirt, partly unbuttoned, tucked into dark gray slacks that stretch over his thick thighs. For half a fraction of a second, I wonder what he looks like beneath his clothes. Are his abs chiseled? "You do remember you signed a contract?"

Yes, and Alexei didn't give me a lot of time to look it over before forcing my signature. It was bad enough he'd barged into my apartment before I could even open the door all the way. I wasn't about to say no. "I'm not backing out. Just curious."

"I'm sure it's nothing you can't handle. Besides, how else would you be able to pay off such a huge debt in one night?" He laughs, lifting an eyebrow. "Unless you'd rather pay it off in one of my other establishments. We aren't as... discerning when it comes to the clientele, but plenty of girls are there who can show you the ropes."

He's talking about a brothel or something like that. So either I can slowly work off my debt and basically be an indentured servant, or I can get it all over with in one night.

What's the worst that could go on down there, anyway? They couldn't let guys torture girls, could they? Cause serious harm, the sort of stuff that means a trip to the hospital or a lawsuit? Think about the liability this seemingly professional guy would bring down on himself if he let that happen.

Besides, I would've heard more than whispered rumors about the club if things got really bad around here. That's not the sort of thing you can get people to shut up about. If a girl got seriously hurt, she'd tell somebody, right? Doubt spurts in my gut, but I squash it before it can develop further. I have to do this. I have no other option.

I realize he's waiting for me to answer, watching me, standing perfectly still. I'd better say something. "No, this is fine."

"I thought so." He picks up the fresh drink, but instead of handing it to me, he sets it on the edge of his desk. Perching on one corner, he folds his arms, looking me up and down again. His face is perfect, to the point where I wonder if he was born with it. He's obviously got the money for it.

But no. The more I look at it, the easier it is to spot the tiny imperfections. A slight tilt to the otherwise straight nose. A faint scar on his square jaw, barely covered by black scruff. Tiny lines at the corners of his eyes. How old is he? Early forties, maybe, though it doesn't show as much on his face as it does in his entire manner. The way he talks, the commanding energy rolling off him.

If there's one thing I learned to pick up on, it's energy. Reading a man, so I'll know whether his silence is just the calm before the storm.

"As per the terms of your contract, you understand that we don't use safe words in Hell. Once you go down there, there's no leaving until the guest is satisfied. Remember that. The satisfaction of my guests is always the highest priority. Tell me you understand that."

"I do. I understand." Still, I can't help myself. "So there's no way to get them to stop?"

His face is blank. "No. Those are the terms. And you did sign a contract, agreeing to those terms."

Yes, I did, because that's my fucking life now. Jumping out a window to escape a burning building, only the street below is also on fire. I can't catch a break.

He tips his head to the side. "It's a funny thing. I can't find much about you online—and yes, before you ask, I make it my business to know who works here, even if it's only for a single night. When I searched for your name online, I barely came up with anything. Do you know how unusual it is for someone your age not to even have social media?"

A cold finger traced an icy path down my spine. "I'm a pretty private person."

"No, I'm a private person. You strike me as someone who's hiding something. Twenty years old and not so much as a Facebook account. That's very unusual. It looks like you've only lived in your apartment a handful of months, but that's the most I could find. And I am very thorough."

What am I supposed to do? Tell him the whole story? Maybe he'll feel sorry for me. I almost snort, doubtful. No, I don't want anybody feeling sorry for me. I was stupid enough to fall for that bastard, stupid enough to believe him every time he said it would never happen again, stupid enough to cover the bruises so nobody would think badly about him.

Getting away, moving to the other side of town, and cutting all ties with Eric was the best decision I ever made. Still, it drained me physically, emotionally, and financially—especially financially. Before I was strong enough to leave him, he drained my bank account and maxed out my credit cards. I was already behind in rent, which meant the only way I could get a new place was with a huge deposit.

"The truth?" He nods. "There's somebody I would rather not see again. Ever."

For one second, I'm afraid he's going to ask for details. He strikes me as the kind of guy who would get off on making a girl relive the memories she would give anything to forget. So long as he could be in control.

Which is why it surprises me when he only nods again. "As long as you're not some undercover vice cop, we're okay."

"Oh, god, no. No, it's not like that. Believe me." I can't help but laugh, which doesn't seem like the right reaction, but it's all I can do. Me, a cop? "I mean, if I was, wouldn't they set me up with a whole online persona to make me look legit?"

He cracks a tiny smile, and I can only think how handsome he'd be if he smiled more instead of looking so serious and stern all the time. "I believe you. And I think you're going to make me a lot of money tonight."

At least one of us is happy about that.

2

ucian

SHE'S NOT what I expected. Nowhere close. Alexei described a weak, shaky, timid girl. Hot, sure, or else she wouldn't be here. When it comes to her face and tight-but-curvy body, she's definitely all he described and more.

It's her spirit that interests me. That little spark in her. Most girls come in here with their shoulders hunched, looking at me from under fake eyelashes, afraid to do more than whisper their name and bob their head up and down when I ask if they're ready to work. Others are simply coked out of their mind, so addicted to drugs that they'll do anything.

This one, though? She looks me right in the eye, stands straight and tall. There's a refreshing sort of honesty about her, but she doesn't overshare. Like that bit about having somebody she doesn't want to see anymore—probably a shady ex-boyfriend or a family member she's running away from.

But she didn't blubber about it. She didn't beg for me to understand her situation, to take mercy and let her out of a contract she didn't thoroughly read. She's direct, to the point, but there's still a thread of vulnerability running through her words. It's enough to get me a little hard, honestly.

Well, it's not the first time I've done business with a girl in a tough situation. That's how most of my employees end up on my doorstep in the first place.

"Here." I pick up the drink I fixed for her and hand it over. "Whiskey rocks. It'll calm your nerves."

Something moves across her face. She doesn't want to admit she's nervous and resents my guessing. "Just take it. Trust me." She extends her hand to accept the drink, and our fingers brush against each other. Her skin is as soft as it looks.

All that discovery does is remind me what's waiting for her in the basement, and something unpleasant stirs north of my dick. I have to look away, finding my own drink and downing what's left. The whiskey sends its usual warmth through me, but it's not enough to loosen my discomfort.

She's perfect, but she won't be for much longer. My hand tightens around the tumbler.

"Would you mind if I have a seat?" She lifts one of her feet, rolling it in a circle. "I'm not used to standing around in shoes like this for so long."

Her frankness teases another smile from me. "Of course. I don't know how women walk in them."

"We do it because men like them." She sits in one of the chairs in front of the desk, crossing her ankles. Demure and ladylike. Again, not like the girls who usually walk through my door. Normally, I don't care much either way—in fact, there's not much profit to be made from modesty.

It's just because she's different. That's all. She's not special. She's just unusual.

I check my watch. He'll be here soon. I should send her downstairs, but something inside me won't let me do it. Not yet. I don't know why.

She must feel the weight of my stare because her fair cheeks go pink an instant before she turns her head, letting a curtain of thick, shining blond hair hide her reaction. But it's too late. I've already seen her blush, and it's like she set a bomb off in my head.

Letting her go through with this is completely fucked up.

I need another drink. Since when do I give a shit either way? She's money on two legs, nothing more. And she owes me. She walked into this with her eyes open. I don't even have to give her this chance to pay off her debt.

So long as I don't think about what she'll look like by the time he's finished with her…

"You better finish that. I pride myself on punctuality as well as discretion." I suck down another whiskey with my back to her, telling myself to forget about it. Adults make decisions, and they have to learn to live with the consequences. That's all there is to it. I don't make the rules.

By the time I turn around, her glass is empty. I take it from her without meeting her gaze, turning away again. I can't look at her.

"Alexei?" The door opens an instant later, the way I knew it would. "Take Rowan down to Hell."

The chair creaks slightly when she stands. "I feel like I should thank you or something…"

She doesn't know it, but that's the worst thing she could possibly say. I have to grit my teeth and will away a rush of something that feels suspiciously like guilt. "Don't bother. Just do what you came here to do. That's all the thanks I need."

Alexei mutters something unintelligible, and Rowan's heels click across the floor. The door closes, leaving me alone.

What the hell is wrong with me? I never get sick, but this must be an exception to the rule because there's no other explanation for how twisted up I suddenly feel inside. That girl has no idea what she has gotten herself into.

But she did get herself into it. She borrowed a lot of money with no means of paying it back, then let the interest build until the amount was in the five-figure range. She signed a contract to pay that debt back, and now she has to live up to the terms she agreed to.

It just so happens some men will pay a lot of money to get what they want. The shit they crave, no matter how twisted it is. So I provide a service in a safe, clean environment.

And Rowan is perfect for him. Alexei was right about that. Skin like alabaster, unblemished. Young, innocent—no way has she ever been in a club like this before, for any reason. Not with those wide, innocent eyes with a hint of fear.

But dammit. Even though she was scared, she didn't flinch. She didn't back down.

And she followed Alexei like a lamb to the slaughter.

"It's not up to me." My voice rings out in the otherwise empty room. There's no one to agree with me, to tell me I'm right. To ease the nagging sense of something being very wrong with this situation.

I've got to get my head screwed on straight. I didn't spend ten years building this business from the ground up to start growing a conscience now. She's just a girl, like every other girl working for me. And once tonight is over, she can go back to her narrow little life.

Glen's kink isn't even the strangest I've ever indulged here. At least that's what I tell myself as I sit behind my desk. I've had clients who were into branding. One burned his name onto a girl's ass, then jerked off onto her wounds after she passed out from the pain. I've had a few who dabbled in vampirism, for lack of a better word. One of them will never be back here again so long as I own the place, the greedy, disgusting fuck.

But Glen? He likes pain. Especially the kind involving knives and bare skin. And he'll just love all that smooth, unscarred skin, too.

People have to live up to their word. Rowan's not the only one who's made promises. Hell-level clients expect freedom and protection, and they pay handsomely for both. I can't go back on that.

Fuck, but I can't stop thinking about her, either.

Alexei's three knocks tell me he's back. "It's done." Meaning his job is finished for now. She's down there, and the fun's about to start. "She's good, right? Like I said?"

"She's good." I can't help but ask my next question since I wasn't precisely paying attention when we first discussed her. "What were the circumstances of your running into each other?"

"She was a waitress at that diner near the college." Yes, more than a few of our short-term employees come from the college. "I was on my way in one night, and I saw her sitting there on the curb, crying. I thought she might be a good prospect. She told me she'd just got fired and would get kicked out of her apartment since she had no money for rent."

He shrugs, grinning. "It was like she was waiting for me. Perfect."

"Perfect." So he loaned her the money she needed, knowing she wouldn't be able to pay it back any more than any of the other girls—and occasionally young men—who eventually end up working in one of my establishments.

Everything is the way it's always been. We have it down to a science by now.

So, why does this feel wrong?

"Have you seen Chloe tonight?" I ask.

He seems surprised by the sudden change in subject. "Yeah, she's on the floor."

"Tell her I want her up here now." He knows better than to ask why.

There's a knock from outside the office a minute later, but still not soon enough. I need something, anything, to distract me.

I press the button, opening the door, and am pleased to find the leggy redhead I requested. She's tried a few different personas over the months she's worked as a stripper down on the main floor and does best as a sexy businesswoman type: buttoned-up blouse, leather pencil skirt, garters, and stockings—the whole nine yards.

No matter how unique men think they are, I've never met one who doesn't respond to a powerful but hot woman. Even I get off on them under the right circumstances, whether or not I'm the one doing the fucking.

"You wanted to see me?" She steps up to the desk, wearing a pleasant smile. It's been a while since I've requested her company, and I already can't wait to watch her at work.

This is who I am. This is what I do. I make money, I provide a service, I get off whenever I feel like it.

I don't think about the girls I use. It's not like they don't get anything out of it.

"I want you to dance for me. Let me see those tits." I lean back in my chair, making myself comfortable as Chloe backs into the center of the office. The music playing downstairs isn't exactly audible, thanks to the soundproofing throughout the building, but the bass comes through.

She uses the beat, swaying her hips while running her hands over her body—ass, hips, tits, then over her face and head. In one quick move, she slides the clip out of her hair, shaking her head to let the red waves fall past her shoulders.

Her fingers work the buttons of her blouse, undoing them one at a time until she reveals a black lace bra barely strong enough to hold back her double-Ds. She massages her tits, pinching her nipples through the lace, and I'm reminded of the perks of my job as my cock stirs.

Perks too valuable to fuck up for any reason.

3

owan

"Take off all your clothes."

That was the only instruction Alexei gave me before closing the door and leaving me alone in this dark basement room. I have no idea what's going on in the other rooms—soundproofing again. The doors were closed as I walked down the hallway, so there was no getting a look inside.

I have no idea what's going to happen down here.

I only know there's a table in the center of the room—a table with straps hanging from the sides, and a light directly above it.

Okay, so the guy likes to restrain his girls. I guess I can deal with that. It's not like I've never felt helpless before, though I wasn't getting paid for it then.

Still, stripping down to bare skin isn't easy. Goose bumps rise up all over my body as I unzip my dress and shimmy out of it. Why bother getting me dressed up if I'll be naked when the client comes in?

No questions. I'm here to do, not to think.

Off comes my bra and panties. I fold them neatly and tuck them inside the dress, hiding them—like at a doctor's appointment. Then, finally, the shoes. My feet thank me for it while my heart pounds loud enough for me to hear it in my head.

I don't know what's worse: the waiting or the dreading what might happen once the waiting's over.

They can't make people do really bad things. They'd never stay in business if they did. Of course, being in this basement room with its black walls and floor and no windows, it's not as easy to believe what I told myself upstairs.

The door creaks open, and I immediately fold my hands in front of my shaved mound. Like it matters. Like he's not going to see all of me if he wants to once I'm strapped down.

The man walks in, and at first sight, my insides feel all loose and shaky.

I don't like this. I don't like him.

And he doesn't like me.

Sure, he smiles, but it's a cold, nasty smile. There's nothing behind his eyes but blank emptiness. I know that emptiness. Eric used to look at me that way before he'd hurt me.

It's like being with him all over again. Only there was never a contract involved back then. I always knew in the back of my mind that he'd never hurt me badly enough for the rest of the world to know what he was capable of.

This guy? I have no idea, and that makes adrenaline rush through my veins. Every instinct screams at me to run, but I can't. Not only because I signed a contract but I'm also completely naked. Where would I go?

"Lie on the table." He takes off his suit jacket and hangs it on a hook near the door. His voice is flat, emotionless. He didn't even ask for my name or anything.

Because I'm not human to him. I'm a thing. Nobody has to tell me for it to be obvious.

When he turns back to me, he's unbuttoning his shirt. He's fit, not even bad-looking, with a nice haircut and polished shoes. But if he approached me on the street, I'd hurry up to get away from him. Everything about the guy screams bad news.

"Are you deaf? On the table." He points at it before unbuttoning his cuffs. "Now. I don't have all night."

I look at the table, lit by that overhead lamp. My blood runs cold. "Do I have to?"

"What?" It's like the sound of a gunshot, and it makes me jump a little. I fold my arms over myself, not to hide but to keep myself from shaking too hard.

"Do I have to get on the table? I mean, we have a whole room, right?" Even though the table's the only thing in the room, really. But the thought of being tied down and defenseless by this man is maybe the worst thing imaginable.

He's not here to have fun. He's here to hurt me. Bad.

"Do I have to call in the bouncers to help me get you into place? I will." He strips off his shirt but stops there, leaving the pants on for now.

I must not answer fast enough since he knocks on the door not a moment later. It opens and in walk two enormous men. He jerks his head toward me without looking my way. "Get her on the table."

I'm going to throw up. They can't. Not if they know what's going to happen in here. They can't be human if they're willing to do what he says without asking questions.

And they are willing.

"No, please, don't do this." It doesn't matter. They don't care that my voice is so high it's practically a squeak. Or that I try my best to fight them off once their huge, rough hands take hold of my arms and legs. Or that I'm close to tears as they force me onto the table, flat on my back.

I twist and turn from one side to the other, but that's no use, either. They don't look at me. They don't say a word. They only hold me down before tying my wrists and ankles tight enough to hurt. I suck in air through my teeth when one of them cinches the last strap, cutting into my skin. Like he's pissed at me for making him do it.

I'm spread-eagle on the table and completely exposed. It's cold in here, making my nipples tight, making me shiver harder than ever. I tug at the restraints, but it's no use. They're too tight and fastened securely to the table.

I'm at his mercy. Oh, god, I'm completely at his mercy, and nobody cares.

The man waits until we're alone again, then shakes his head slowly. "You've already wasted my time. You're lucky you look so good when you're struggling." Holy shit, he's hard, like to the point where his dick is jutting out in front of him as he walks slowly around the table.

He comes to a stop at my feet, and I raise my head slightly so I can see him. As much as I don't want to look at him, I'm afraid to close my eyes. Afraid of what'll happen without my knowing it's coming.

So I'm treated to the sight of him rubbing his bulge, eyes now half-lidded as they travel over every inch of my body. "So perfect," he breathes while his hand moves. "Where's he been keeping you? I have half a mind to complain that we're only making each other's acquaintances now."

Acquaintance. That word stirs something in my brain, and all the crime movies and shows I've ever watched come back to me at once. If he thinks of me as a person, he might be less ready to hurt me. I have to try.

"My name is Rowan. What's your name?" God, it's fucking impossible to keep my voice from shaking. I hate how weak and scared I sound, mostly because I know he's getting off on it. His hand is moving faster, his breathing picking up.

"I don't remember asking for your name. And I don't care what it is." He walks slowly up the length of the table, unzipping his pants. I don't want to see what he pulls out, but I can't help myself. I need to know what he's going to put inside me.

Oh fuck, he's going to be inside me. This sick, twisted piece of shit. He hasn't laid a finger on me yet, but I know this isn't where our night together will end. He's not satisfied to look at me or know how completely terrified I am.

It's like he can read my mind. "You think this is bad?" It's almost a sigh, almost gentle. "You think this is the worst that's going to happen to you tonight? Oh, no. We haven't even gotten started."

Suddenly, he reaches out, taking my right nipple between his thumb and forefinger. When he pinches brutally hard, I let out a yelp that only makes him tighten his grip. It's like he wants to tear it off me.

"Please, stop! Stop!" I squeeze my eyes shut and beg myself not to cry, but I can feel the tears welling up, and oh, god, he's laughing. I'm struggling not to cry as he's practically tearing my nipple off, and he's laughing.

Somebody's got to be watching, right? They must have cameras around here. No way a guy like Lucian—in control, powerful, rich—would let anything happen without him knowing about it and being able to watch.

When I open my eyes, I look around, desperate, hoping to see a tiny red dot in a corner or something. Anything that will give away the presence of a camera. "Please, I can't do this. Let me out of here. I'm begging you."

"Who are you talking to?" He finally lets go of me, and the tears start flowing, more out of relief than anything else. They soak into my hair and leave trails down the sides of my face. "Nobody can hear you. Nobody can see you. Only me."

In a swift move, he leans down, leaving maybe an inch between our faces. I twist my head away, but he grabs my jaw and squeezes, turning my face back to him.

Those empty, soulless eyes bore into me. I grit my teeth to hold back the whimpers threatening to get out.

"And I'm not about to let you go anywhere," he whispers. "So don't waste your breath." His fingers dig into my jaw, harder all the time. I can barely keep from crying out.

It's like with Eric. I used to try so hard to stay quiet so he wouldn't have the satisfaction of hearing me cry.

Except this sick piece of shit seems to like that. "You're a tough one." When he smiles, I start trembling—and this time, I can't control it. "But you'll break. They always do once I really get going. I'll remember you fondly for a long time. Believe me."

Like I care. Like I want him to.

Like I don't already want to forget ever setting eyes on him.

He releases my jaw before continuing his slow walk around the table. I twist my hands around, trying to reach the buckles on the restraints, but it's no use. It's like being in a nightmare I can't wake up from. The worst nightmare I've ever had.

Only there's no actual pain in a nightmare.

When he climbs onto the table between my spread legs, I'm almost glad. He'll fuck me and get it over with. Maybe he'll be rough, but it won't last forever. I'll get through this.

"So perfect. Such smooth, soft skin." He drags a hand over my calf, my thigh as he moves over my body. I have to take a deep breath to hold back the bile rising in my throat. A shudder of revulsion runs through me, which only makes him chuckle.

It'll be over soon. He's practically ready to come now. Yes, there's precum dripping from the head of his substantial cock, now poised over my pussy. It won't take long. It'll be over soon.

Only he doesn't shove his way inside me.

He doesn't even touch me down there.

Instead, he straddles my hips, one leg on either side. I wonder if he plans on fucking my face or my tits or what. I don't care, so long as he finishes. My heart's about to pound out of my chest, and cold sweat is now rolling down the back of my neck.

It's the waiting. The not knowing. That's the worst part.

And he knows that, too, which is why he's smiling as he strokes his dripping cock, poised over top of me. "Now, it's time to really have some fun."

Which is when he uses his free hand to reach into his back pocket and pulls out a switchblade.

All the air in my lungs leaves in one huge exhale, like somebody punched me in the stomach with all their might. He didn't punch me, but he might as well have.

"No. No, no, no way." My body takes over for me, bucking off the table. I barely feel the pain in my shoulders as I jerk my arms harder than ever.

He smiles wider than ever. "Shh. It'll be over soon."

"No! What do you think you're doing with that?" I watch in horror as he lowers the blade a little at a time. The light glints off it, blinding me, but I can't take my eyes off it.

He sounds genuinely happy when he laughs. "Wait and see, bitch." The blade touches the right side of my chest above my bruised nipple.

Then it presses. Harder. Until blood seeps from under it.

Instinct must be what freezes me solid—he could stab me for real if I keep bucking up and down. All I can do is watch in shock as he drags the blade from right to left, splitting the skin open, leaving a dark red line behind it.

I don't beg or plead this time.

All I can do is scream—loud, long, high-pitched—while I fight like I've never fought in my life. My shoulders, my arms, my wrists feel like they're going to break. My feet pound the table, and my head swings back and forth. He's going to slice me open. I can't let him do this, and nobody's coming to help me.

"That's right." He's laughing softly, jerking himself off, raising the knife again. "Keep fighting, bitch. I'm just getting started. We'll see how long before you give up."

4

ucian

Chloe's long gone, having done her job admirably as always. When it comes to the regular employees—my dancers, for instance—nothing but the best will do. Still, some of them manage to stand out from the crowd either thanks to looks or talent. Chloe has both.

Though she wasn't enough to get me out of my head. I'm no closer to forgetting that girl in the basement than I was before. She's like an itch deep under my skin, one I could scratch until I draw blood but be no closer to satisfying.

At this rate, I'd bleed to death, but I wouldn't be rid of her. The way she stood here, frank and brave. I'm no pushover, and I lost count a long time ago of the number of girls I've reduced to tears in this very office.

Not her. Not Rowan.

Goddammit.

You know you can't do this. I've been a hard-ass all these years, insisting on strict adherence to the rules. I've been merciless when it comes to firing employees for even the slightest offense.

Years ago, I heard an anecdote relating to human psychology. It had to do with the decline of a neighborhood stemming from a single broken window. That's all it takes to get the ball rolling. If that window goes unfixed, eventually, there'll be another. A neighbor will neglect to mow their lawn, another will stop picking up after their dog.

I took it to heart. It's how I run my business. If one person gets away with an infraction, that will only encourage others to be lax, show up late, step over the line, and become too deeply intimate with their customers. I might be an asshole about the rules, but this isn't a business that tolerates the undisciplined.

Well, it does, but not in establishments like mine. More than once, I've advised an employee to find some backwoods stripper bar if she wants to act like a sloppy slut.

Here, we practice discretion, which requires discipline. It takes discipline to properly serve customers, as well. Taking them to their breaking point and beyond without actually breaking them.

No one can ever say I don't treat my employees well. I'm not that much of an asshole. All things considered. I've even practiced generosity with Rowan. I'll barely make a profit once her debt's clear.

Instead, I want her to stop working. I don't want him to put his hands on her, though I'm sure that's already happened. He's probably marring her unblemished skin as I'm sitting here. The thought makes me sick.

What sort of hypocrite would I be if I turned my back on the rules I've driven into the skulls of everyone who's ever stepped through my door?

Do I care?

I'm out of my chair and in the hall before there's time to convince myself what a completely fucked-up idea this is. Maybe the biggest mistake I've ever made. Unfortunately, that's not enough to stop me from taking the back stairs straight to Hell.

The bouncers waiting in front of the doors lining both sides of the long hallway stand a little straighter when they see me coming. This is hardly my first visit, but I don't make a point of visiting Hell often. Special occasions come up every now and then, but for the most part, I don't mix with the fucked-up kinks we indulge down here.

Even I have limits when it comes to what I can stomach.

Glen's room sits at the end of the hall, furthest from the stairs. I eyeball the pair guarding the room, both of whom stand with hands folded in front of them, their backs to the wall. "I'm going in there."

Poor bastards don't know what to do. They know as well as I do what a massive breach of protocol I'm describing. One of the conditions of the job entails staying out of the room no matter what they hear. These aren't your typical guys off the street who only think they're hard-asses because they've been breaking legs since dropping out of high school.

"Boss, are you sure?" They exchange a look. "He's not gonna like it."

"Are you more concerned with what he likes or what I like?" My unblinking eyes move from one of them to the other. "Because you're welcome to work for him starting tomorrow if that's how you feel about it. Now open the fucking door."

One of them opens his mouth instead of the door, but it's not his voice I hear.

It's Rowan's. And she's screaming.

"Now." When neither of the useless bastards moves fast enough, I push past them and throw the door open.

What I see on the other side turns my stomach. She's under him, spread-eagle, tied down and bleeding.

It's not the blood that disturbs me. It's the terror on her face, in her eyes when her head swings my way. Her face is slick with tears, eye makeup running down her cheeks and temples. She's been weeping and screaming, and the sick fuck on top of her is the reason.

I adjust my cuffs, focusing my gaze on them rather than looking at what's in front of me. I might do something I can't undo otherwise. "There's been a change in plans."

He's straddling her with the knife in his hand. "What?"

I make it a point not to look at the erection jutting out from his open fly. "We've had to change plans." I gesture to the pair behind me. "Escort our guest to room four. He'll find a new companion there."

"But I want this one."

"I understand, and I ask your forgiveness for this mix-up." I hold his gaze, unflinching. "Naturally, we'll refund you for the inconvenience. Your next companion is on the house."

He doesn't move, though he's at least started to soften. Rowan, on the other hand, hasn't stopped hyperventilating. Even though Glen's not paying attention to her anymore, she can't take her eyes off the blade. Blood trickles in a thin line from the cut on her chest down over her side.

There's something stark, startling about the sight of a red line over her perfect skin. The light hanging over the table only highlights the contrast. It draws my eye.

Glen needs to get out of here before I kill him.

He takes his time about climbing down from the table, muttering things about professionalism and contracts. But he doesn't argue—that's key. The man knows there isn't anywhere else in town or even within a reasonable driving distance where he'd be able to satisfy his unique needs.

And once I ask a customer not to return, no matter how long they've been a visitor, they don't cross the threshold again for any reason. They could be bleeding to death on the sidewalk, and I would call for an ambulance, but I wouldn't bring them inside.

It takes a lot for me to get to that point, and I've only had to do it twice. After all, a contract is a contract, and I have to hold up my end of the bargain.

Unless Glen plays it smart, he's about to become number three.

Lucky for him, he plays it smart. My guys flank him on the way out the door, though, just in case he decides to change his mind. I wouldn't necessarily put it past him—one of those buttoned-up types on the street and a complete psycho in his private life.

No, he's smart. He doesn't want to have to hunt his victims on the streets.

I turn to Rowan as the door closes, leaving us alone. "Oh, my god." Her chest heaves as she sobs, tears soaking her face and her hair. "Oh, my god, please. Please, let me go. Thank you for making him stop. Please, let me go." She turns her wrists back and forth in the cuffs, and I notice how red and chafed they are. Ankles, too. She's been struggling.

Goddammit. Glen's not the only one who gets off on a helpless woman. If this were any other situation, the things I'd do to her.

My cock stirs at the mere thought of it. Even her begging turns me on. It adds to the helplessness, makes it more authentic.

In her case, it is authentic. She's not playing. The extra desperation in her voice, in the way she struggles even though she doesn't have a hope of escaping, makes me want to savor this moment. It makes me want to savor her.

What I could do to this woman. What I could make her do to me. Do for me. The need to possess her consumes me.

Now I know it won't be enough to let her go. I want her for myself. I want her to please me, to work off her debt with me. Because no matter how upset she is and no matter how freaked out Glen made her, she still owes me.

I'm not a perfect man. I know there's darkness in me. I don't bother trying to fight it—it'd be a waste of time, like fighting my need for air and water or willing my eyes into changing color. I don't believe in wasting time. In wishing.

And the darkness in me flares to life, threatening to overtake me now. Something in this girl speaks to that part of me. Sings to it. Entices it, teases it, invites it to come out and play. I've never known a temptation this sweet. A man could become addicted.

"I relate to the people who visit this club. Men and women both." I make it a point to keep my voice low so as not to upset her further. She's been through enough tonight. Besides, I need her to hear me, and if she's sobbing and blubbering, there's no chance of that.

She's watching me now, weeping softly. "Let me go." Her voice is like that of a wounded child. There's none of that bravery from up in my office. It didn't take much to break her, did it? A few shallow cuts.

Though I can imagine her horror, still. I try not to relate to the girls who come here to work, but there are times when I can't help it. "I imagine this evening was difficult for you. I can't help what my customers want. I only provide an outlet for their darkest desires. I like to imagine this keeps them from indulging elsewhere, under less controlled circumstances."

Either she's unimpressed, or she's too busy trying to understand where this is going to offer any meaningful response. All she does is whimper, her struggles weakening. She's exhausted herself.

"You have to understand something, Rowan." I walk a slow circle around the table, taking in every inch of her. Imagining the many positions I can twist her supple body into. "I believe in fairness. In people living up to their promises and obligations. Tonight was too much for you. I thought it would be."

Her whimpering grows slightly louder.

"I wouldn't break the rules for just anybody. In fact, this is the first time I've stopped a customer before they reached satisfaction. I hope you know what that means."

She lifts her head, eyes finding mine. "Thank you?"

I can't tell whether she's genuinely thanking me or making an ironic comment, and I like that. The fact of her not being entirely transparent. Just enough to keep me intrigued.

"However." I come to a stop between her legs. She's delectable: smooth-shaven, plump lips that ought to glisten with my cum. I force my eyes away from the sight. "As difficult as this evening was for you, your debt still stands."

Her eyes go perfectly round an instant before her mouth falls open. "Oh, no, please! I can't. I can't go through this again, please. I'll do anything else."

"You're right. You will do something else."

Her panicked breathing only slows slightly. "Wh-what do you want instead?" she asks in a voice that's more like a squeak.

"You will return to the club four times." When she pulls in a breath, ready to start begging again, I hold up a hand. "I'm not finished. You'll return four times, and we'll play out my kink."

Her delicate brows knit together. "You and me?"

"Don't make assumptions." I lift a shoulder. "Otherwise, my brothel is one of the finest in the tri-state area... but it's still a brothel. The choice is yours. Let me remind you, though, that the debt will be paid one way or another."

Then a wave of generosity washes over me. "I'll include an extra ten thousand dollars for you as payment."

"I'll do it," she blurts out nearly before I finish the sentence.

Something told me that would help her decide.

5

Rowan

Here I am again. And I still have no idea what the hell I'm getting into.

He didn't tell me how to dress this time, something I didn't realize until after I got home. After I sat in a hot bathtub long enough that my fingers pruned, and the water went cold. And still, I sat there, knees drawn up to my chest, my arms wrapped around them. I didn't keep track of time. It could've been hours, for all I know.

Even after all that, I didn't feel clean when I got out.

That guy with the knife, whatever his name is, didn't hurt me as badly as he could have. I know that. The cut on my chest is shallow, hardly anything, really. Just enough to draw blood. I've had worse from a pissed-off cat. That cut wasn't the scary part. It was the possibility of what could have happened. It was me being utterly helpless.

Even more helpless than I had been with Eric. It was the look in that guy's eyes.

Something tells me he wasn't taking pity on me, that psycho. He was only warming up, testing my reaction. I hope he got what he wanted. And I can't help but wonder who he ended up going to after me, who Lucian sent him to. What's that girl's story? How did she end up in Hell, and did she make it back out in one piece?

The name makes me snicker darkly as I walk to the door. Whoever was in charge of naming the levels in the club knew what they were doing because I got a glimpse of hell last night. Not my first glimpse, and probably not my last.

I hope the more modest dress I chose for tonight is okay. I get the feeling that if it mattered, Lucian would've said something. It's not like we spent a lot of time together, so I haven't gotten a total read on him yet, but he strikes me as somebody who controls everything he possibly can. Everything that matters, anyway.

If he didn't mention it, I doubt it matters.

Besides, something tells me I won't be wearing clothes for long. It was one thing to wear what I wore last night so he could get an idea of how I look and whether I was worth the asking price.

Now? He's seen every inch of me. I shudder at the memory of that table, being strapped down and completely helpless. Maybe it's the fact that he didn't touch me. Maybe that's why I came back tonight. He didn't take advantage of me when I was right there—his for the taking.

Not that I have much of a choice. I had to come back, especially since ten thousand bucks magically appeared in my checking account this morning when I checked online. How it got there so quickly, I have no idea. I only know it's there, so he's fulfilled his part of the bargain. That means it's time for me to fulfill my part.

I could've tried to run away. Ten grand can put a lot of distance between a girl and the shit she wants to get away from. But if the man could afford to wire me that much money on a whim, something tells me he could find me if he felt like it.

Nobody is waiting for me outside tonight. I open the door and let myself in, peering through the near darkness. I'm early, and it looks like only one or two customers have come in before me. A pair of men are sitting at the bar in the room beyond the entrance, and a few mostly naked girls walk around.

"Can I help you?"

I have to keep myself from jumping in surprise at the sudden voice coming from beside me. The girl is beautiful, with glowing ebony skin, wearing only a see-through bra and thong. I feel like yesterday's leftovers all of a sudden, which is ridiculous since I'm not even trying to compete with her or any of the girls who work here.

"I think so? Um, I'm here to see Lucian. He asked me to come back tonight."

"He's right there." She nods toward the bar, and now I realize what I missed before. One of the men sitting at the bar, sipping on something in a rocks glass, is Lucian. I didn't imagine he would ever socialize with his customers, but then who knows if the guy's actually a customer? It's not my business, anyway.

And I don't really care, either—it's a defense mechanism, trying to distract myself by fixing my attention on random things. Trying to make sense of them so I don't have to make sense of the nightmare running through my head.

It's something I've had a lot of practice with.

I walk slowly from the reception area, my head held high. I won't let him break me down—as it is, I'm ashamed of how I acted last night. How I whimpered and begged him.

Though deep down, I think it turned him on. It makes me wonder for maybe the millionth time since he told me to come back just what his kink is. He never did say. I really wish he had now.

What if it's the same as what happened to me last night? I don't know if I could live through that again without losing my mind.

He sees me and finishes his drink before murmuring something to the man sitting beside him. I can't get a read on that one, and now I hope he's not going to be a part of what happens tonight. I didn't sign on for a gang bang. Then again, I don't know what I signed on for. I just want to get it over with.

"You came." There's no surprise in his voice. In fact, there's not much of anything. He's stating the facts, that's all.

"Did I have a choice?"

The corner of his mouth slides upward. "No. You didn't." He gestures with his hand, waving me on without saying another word.

We walk more slowly this time, so I can get a better look at the main floor. "This is really beautiful." And it is. I'm not just saying that to kiss up to him or convince him to take it easier on me. This isn't what I would've imagined a sex club looking like. It's very sleek, luxurious, and I guess it should be considering how much people probably pay to live out their fantasies here.

I wonder how much that sadistic bastard from last night pays. Definitely enough to help afford the top-shelf liquor at the bar.

If Lucian heard me compliment his establishment, he chooses not to respond. So is this the game we're playing? That's fine. I can play the quiet game.

We come to the stairs. One set leads up, one leads down.

Now fear starts to trace a cold line up my spine. Are we going to Heaven or to Hell? Did I sign up for more of what I've already gone through? *Please, please, go upstairs. Go upstairs.*

I practically have to lean against the wall for support when Lucian does, thank god, go up the stairs. If it's happening in Heaven, I can handle it. Or so I want to believe, anyway.

"This way." He takes me past the hall on our right, the one leading to his office, and leads me deeper down the main hall extending in front of us and cutting down the center of the floor. Some of the rooms are open, without even any doors, so people passing by can look inside and watch the festivities. I hear soft moaning coming from one of the rooms, and curiosity makes me sneak a look from the corner of my eye.

"Do you like that?" I realize Lucian fell in step beside me rather than walking ahead of me, and he's been watching my reaction.

"I didn't really get a good look," I confess, and I'm glad the few sconces on the walls don't give off much light. So he can't see the heated flush on my cheeks.

"By all means. They wouldn't perform in the open if they didn't want to be watched." He gestures toward the doorway, and I get the feeling I shouldn't say no.

There are three people in there: a man lying on his back across a leather-covered bench, dressed in a shiny rubber suit from head to toe. A leather-clad woman is playing with his dick, smacking it around while he moans from behind his mask. A second man watches from the corner, stroking himself while instructing the woman to be rougher.

"Do you like what you see?" Lucian's breath is hot on the back of my neck, yet it makes me shiver. I can't say I do, but I nod anyway. I've never understood shaming or hurting somebody to get off, but I know there are people who want nothing more than to be abused.

Maybe that's his kink. Or maybe he likes to watch and identifies with the guy in the corner. I could handle that. Is that why he wanted me to stop here, to watch for a minute? Is he introducing me to what he wants for tonight?

No, as it turns out. "This way." He continues down the hall and opens the door to one of the other rooms.

I can't stop shaking. I walk with my arms wrapped around myself, afraid of what I'll find. Another table with restraints? Something worse than that?

All I find is what looks like any ordinary bedroom: a double bed with lots of pillows, soft lighting from lamps on either side. Off to the left is another room, its door open—just a bathroom, plain and simple. I keep waiting for something or somebody to jump out at me. But it doesn't happen. Lucian closes the door, sealing off any noise traveling from those open rooms.

I can hear my heart pounding as I turned to him. "What do you want from me?"

He looks just as impeccable as he did last night, but there's something different about him, just the same. A light in his eyes, the tensing of his jaw as he looks me up and down. The slight flaring of his nostrils. I got very good at reading body language, thanks to Eric.

And everything about Lucian tells me something is simmering below the surface.

"Tonight, you're all mine." He begins unbuttoning his suit jacket, his eyes on me as he slides it from his shoulders. The tie comes next, and I wonder if he will use it as a blindfold or a restraint. "I want you to fight me."

For one brief, insane moment, I imagine us sparring with gloves. But, something tells me that's not what he means. "Fight you?" I whisper.

"Yes. Pretend you don't want this."

Pretend? I don't think that will be too hard since there won't be any pretending about it. Maybe if this was a different situation and we had met someplace else, it would be different. There's no denying how hot he is, how handsome and sexy. His whole aura is sexual, sensual, but also confident and commanding. It's a brutal combination that might melt me otherwise.

But I'm not in this situation because I want to be.

"And that's it?" I can't help but ask. My voice is so small, and I wish I didn't sound so scared. Though something tells me he gets off on that, too. Or else he wouldn't want to pretend to force himself on me.

"It will be, so long as you do what I ask." He takes a step closer, then another, extending one hand. "Come here." It's not an invitation. It's an order. Still, there's enough honey in his voice to make me think this might not be so bad. Definitely better than being tied down and cut to pieces.

So I take his hand, noticing how small it is compared to his. He engulfs me, closing his fingers around mine, and a slight tug leads me to the foot of the bed. The duvet is sumptuous, silk, and I have to resist the impulse to run my hands over it as I sit.

He stands in front of me, parting my legs with one knee and positioning himself between them. I look up at him and have to remind myself to breathe as my heart picks up speed again.

He strokes my hair, and his touch is surprisingly gentle. "You're perfect."

Before I can thank him for the compliment, his gentle hand turns into a fist, wrapping my hair around it and pulling my head forward. I can't even take a breath before my face is pressed against his crotch through his pants.

"You're going to feel this cock inside you." He moves his hips, grinding himself against my face. "In your mouth. Your cunt. There's nothing you can do about it."

I'm supposed to fight, so I try to pull my face away. When his grip only tightens, I yank on his wrist while trying to push him away with the other hand.

He chuckles, pulling me in harder. "Come on. You can do more than that, can't you?" Since I can't say anything, I beat at his hand and try like hell to turn my face away from his growing bulge.

He pulls my hair, tipping my head back. I can breathe now, and I gulp down as much air as possible while he unzips his pants with his other hand. He's breathing heavy, looking down at me with his eyes half-lidded.

The next thing I know, he pulls me in again, and this time he guides himself into my mouth and plunges deep with one solid thrust.

Immediately, I gag when he hits the back of my throat, but he only pushes in even farther. I don't have to remind myself to fight as I'm afraid I'll choke to death if I don't. I try to push him away, beating my fists against his thighs, and he chuckles darkly before pulling back and slamming himself into me again.

My nose is against his pubic bone, and I can't breathe. He's suffocating me, fucking my face so hard his balls slap my chin, and tears roll down my cheeks. I can barely pull in any air, and I can feel myself getting light-headed as he drives into me over and over.

I don't have to tell myself to fight. Reflex is doing that for me, my body taking over, fighting to make sure it stays alive. It's not working, though. He's not letting up—if anything, he takes me harder, his thrusts sharper.

When he finally yanks my head back, I could cry with relief, even though the hand in my hair hurts like hell. I'm sweating and tearstained and gasping for air.

He smiles—nasty, cold, pleased, before pushing me back onto the bed.

Reflex takes over again, and I try to slap his hands away as he reaches under my dress. "That's right," he grunts. "Try to stop me. See what good it does." He clamps his hands around my wrists and pulls my arms over my head, then pins them down with one hand while fishing under my dress again.

I wriggle back and forth, grunting and whimpering and panting for air, genuinely trying to escape this. He's enormous—my mouth and throat hurt from taking him—and I've never put anything that big inside me before.

I barely hear the tearing of my panties over the blood rushing in my ears. There's no closing my legs to him, not when he's already wedging himself between my thighs. He presses against my entrance for a split second before shoving his dick inside me.

I bite my lip against the cry of discomfort-bordering-on-pain as he stretches me beyond what I've felt before. "So tight." I look up in time to see him close his eyes, his mouth an O-shape.

He lets go of my wrists and straightens up so he can take off his shirt. I almost forget I'm supposed to be fighting, too busy staring at his chiseled chest and torso, his thick arms and shoulders. His hips don't let up, pumping, taking me hard.

And oh, my god. There's warmth down there, in my core, at the place where our bodies are connected. Heat. I'm getting wet. This is making me wet. What the hell is wrong with me? Am I broken or something?

I only know that if this keeps going much longer, I'm going to come.

6

Lucian

I CAN'T BELIEVE how perfect she is. So tight, gripping me, pulling me deeper.

Submissive but fighting at the same time. Willing to do what I want. Wide-eyed, brave, and innocent.

When I take her by the throat and squeeze, still pumping in and out, she tries to push my hand away, tries to turn her face from mine. Just the way I want her to. Whether she's faking for my sake or not, it doesn't matter. The effect is the same, and it's pushing all my buttons.

It's like she was meant for me. Built exclusively for my pleasure.

"That's right," I groan, holding her tighter. "Try to fight me. It's no use. You only make me want to break you when you do that." Her eyes widen in response, and I can't help but laugh.

I pull out, though it's the last thing I want to do, and for a moment, she looks relieved. Like it's over. I let her think that for a moment, stroking myself, looking down at her. "Don't pretend you didn't get wet," I whisper, and the shame that washes over her face makes me harder than ever. I have to slow my strokes when instinct would have me stroke faster, my release just over the horizon.

No way am I ending this yet. Not when there's so much more to explore.

"Don't pretend you aren't a little slut." I take her by one leg and flip her over, baring her ass to me. A creamy, tight little ass, the sort of ass a man could fall to his knees and worship. When I strike it with my palm, she yelps, which only earns her another strike, hard enough to make her flesh jiggle. "Don't pretend you aren't enjoying this."

She tries to push herself up on her palms like she wants to get away, but one firm hand in the center of her back reminds her who's in charge. I hold her down while, with the other hand, I guide myself back into her tight tunnel.

Yes, she definitely got wet. She's wetter still, so slick. I close my eyes and savor the sensation, sinking deep.

"You're my little slut now," I grunt between thrusts, driving her into the mattress every time my body meets hers. "This pussy is mine. This ass is mine. Whenever I want it. You belong to me." When she tries to resist, scrambling to crawl away from me, I only take her harder.

She lets out a yelp when I grab her by the wrists, bending her arms, twisting them until her hands are pinned behind her back. "Is this how you want it?" I ask, using my other hand to pull her head back by the hair. "Do you like it this way, my little slut? Being used like this? Is that what's making you drip?"

She's almost beyond speaking, letting out a high-pitched cry in time with every brutal thrust. "Please... Please..." It's halfway between a moan and a sob.

"Please, what? You think you get to ask favors now? You think it matters what you want?" I yank her hair a little harder before shoving her face down into the mattress. "You don't get to speak. You're here to get fucked."

It's not the way she moans that surprises me. It's the flutter of her inner walls. I'm not imagining this. She's squeezing me so tightly I have to force myself in and out. Almost like she's—

She squeals, shudders, and her muscles ripple around my shaft. Holy shit. Is she coming? She is, and I can't resist the way she milks me, holding me in place. I have no choice but to let go, groaning in satisfaction while spurting my cum deep inside her cunt.

It only takes a second for me to come back to my senses, and I pull my cock from her. Too late now. My cum drips out of her, soaking into the silk duvet. I didn't use a condom. Fuck me. What was I thinking?

I wasn't thinking. This girl is dangerous. She makes me forget everything I know—all of the rules I've set for myself and for my business.

She hasn't moved, save for some trembling from her legs. Her breath comes in ragged gasps, and her face is still turned away from me, half-hidden. What's she feeling now? Shame, most likely, since I doubt she imagined herself capable of coming in a situation like the one I put her in. I'm sure she sees herself as a good girl, beyond the depravity I've made my stock and trade.

Now she knows the truth about herself, and so do I. The girl has hidden depths. I can't help but want to explore them.

This isn't the time for that. I remind myself of the agreement we made. No, there was nothing in that agreement about a second go-round per visit—in fact, we never got into specifics. I'm not such a cold-hearted monster as that. I won't take advantage of her for not knowing enough to ask for specific terms.

I go to the attached bathroom and wet a washcloth, cleaning what's left of her off my cock. All the while, I keep part of my attention on her, but she's still facedown on the bed. She's breathing, though, her back rising and falling evenly.

I gather myself together, taking my time, savoring the sight of her. Used, dripping cum, broken. I already know I'll want her again, and again after that. This was one of the four agreed-upon encounters, leaving me three more. I don't know if that will be enough. There are so many things I want to do to her. So many fantasies I want to play out.

Once I'm dressed, I wet another cloth with warm water and bring it to her. "Rollover," I command, but my voice no longer carries the edge it did only minutes ago. She does as she's told, eyes closed, her face still turned away. At the touch of the warm cloth, she flinches, her thighs closing around my hand. "Relax. The fun is over...for now." I think I hear her snort as if she finds what I said funny. Sarcasm?

Considering the fact that she came on my cock, I don't think she has much room to be sarcastic.

Once I'm finished, I take the cloth back to the bathroom and toss it in the hamper beneath the sink for one of the girls to pick up later, after closing. "Get dressed."

I turn to face her in time to see her sit up, moving slowly, wincing as she rolls her shoulders, flexes her arms. There are scraps of fabric underneath her, which I realize are her ruined panties. Cheap things, easily torn. She frowns briefly but says nothing, leaving them aside before standing. I'm sure she can afford more, thanks to the ten thousand I made sure transferred to her account earlier today.

What is it about her? Everything she does fascinates me. She's hardly the first woman I've taken the way I took her, certainly not the first with debt in need of paying off. That's one of Alexei's primary jobs, making sure there are plenty of young women indebted to our organization.

I've had many of them, in whatever way happened to suit me at the time. And I've left them in various states of disarray—sweat-slick, makeup ruined, hair a rat's nest, clothes rumpled or torn.

Never before have I lingered, watching one of those women pull herself together afterward. Once I'm finished, that's it. There are other things to do. The same is true tonight, but my feet seem to have grown roots. I can't move.

I clear my throat, noting the way she jumps at the sound. "There will be a car waiting for you downstairs. The driver knows where you live and will take you there." I have to get out of here. There's work to be done, for one thing. For another, the longer I stay, the more I'm going to want to talk to her. That's the last thing either of us needs.

Her head bobs up and down, hands clasped in front of her. Nobody looking at her now would guess how she just got fucked, and how much she enjoyed it. Her eyes are downcast, focused on the toes of my shoes.

Before I can cross the room and open the door, she lifts her head slightly. "When should I come back?" she murmurs, her eyes shaded by the hair cascading in front of her face.

I consider this, studying her as I do. I'm tempted to tell her to return tomorrow, but that would be childish and undisciplined. I can't use up my visits all at once, no matter how much I want to.

Besides, that would be too easy for her. I don't want that, either. In fact, now that I think about it, I enjoy the idea of her not knowing exactly when I'll reappear in her life. Living in her brain the way she'll live in mine.

"Next time, you won't come to me," I decide. "I'll come to you."

"When?" And then, as if she thinks twice about her boldness, she lowers her head again. "Just so I can be ready."

"It might be a better idea to keep yourself ready for me. When I decide to come for you, it will be a surprise. You'll be given no warning. Be ready. I don't react well to disappointment, Rowan."

She nods. "Okay. I'll be ready for you." And damned if the thought of that doesn't make my cock stir as I leave her, striding down the hall past rooms now much busier than they were when I first came upstairs.

It will be another busy night, and a profitable one at that.

And I know even before I reach my office that the rest of my evening will be spent thinking of her.

7

Rowan

Three days after my night with Lucian, and my thighs have finally stopped aching when I walk.

The shame, though? That hasn't gone anywhere. If anything, the more I think about that night, the more ashamed I feel. There was no reason I should've gotten off on that. It doesn't matter that my reaction was completely involuntary. I still feel like my body betrayed me, and I can only guess what he must think of me.

I even tried to stop it from happening, but it was no use. I still can't figure out what that says about me. I should've been disgusted, horrified, and on some level, I was. I couldn't tell how much he said and did was for show and how much was sincere. Maybe all of it was. Maybe the real Lucian is the one I saw in that little room when it was just the two of us.

The worst part is, I can't even pretend I don't want to see him again.

It makes no sense. And I've tried to figure it out. God knows I have. No matter how I try to distract myself with day-to-day life, memories pop up out of nowhere when I least expect them.

His hand around my throat. Smacking my ass. Forcing me to suck his dick, practically smothering me, almost choking me.

I should want to shove those memories away with both hands and turn my back on them.

So why does it always get me a little wet when I remember the way he handled me? Why does my heart start to race?

One thing is for sure: I've never taken such a level of interest in my personal grooming. Not while I was single, anyway. Even Eric didn't expect me to be clean-shaven all the time, smooth and perfect. Hell, when he wanted me, it didn't matter what condition or mood I was in.

Now, every day since I left the club, I make sure to carefully shave all over. I wear my best underwear, too, even if it might end up getting ruined. I've made sure to do my hair and put on a little makeup, even if I don't expect to do anything more than sit around my crummy little apartment. Waiting. Wondering.

For all I know, he's getting off on this, too. Knowing he has this control over me, that I bathe, groom and dress with him in mind. How much longer will it be before he comes for me? I have no idea, just like I have no idea what he's going to do when he does.

Another fantasy like the one we acted out the other night? Maybe this time, he'll break in and pretend to be an intruder. I guess he'll want me to fight back again.

I can't spend all of my time thinking about this. There's so much more I need to do. At the top of the list? Finding a new job. At least there's no real urgency now—the extra ten thousand is a nice cushion, a much bigger cushion than I've ever had. There's more money in my bank account right now than there's ever been at one time. I can't shake the feeling that I'm rich, even though I know I'm not really. People like Lucian are rich. I only have a nest egg.

I would like it to stay that way. It would be good to keep a lot of that money where it is, just in case. So I never have to put myself in a position like this again, with somebody else holding all the cards. Controlling my life, my decisions. I won't be weak anymore.

I remember so clearly being little and sitting at the breakfast table with my mom, with her spreading the classified section of the newspaper in front of her and circling jobs that looked promising. Even back then, people were starting to post jobs on the internet, but we didn't have a computer. We couldn't afford one.

Now I can sit on my sofa and scroll through ads for jobs using my phone. It's funny how the world changes. I'm sure if Mom were still here, she would refuse to upgrade her old flip phone.

There isn't too much I'm qualified to do. Waitressing, working behind a counter. It looks like there are a few spots open in the big chain restaurants scattered around the mall downtown, and I consider applying for them. A craft store is looking for help with stocking shelves, but they want people who can easily lift twenty-five pounds, and I'm not sure I can manage that. I wonder if there's anything around the apartment that weighs that much, so I can try it out.

I briefly entertain the idea of calling Eve, my best friend. Her stepbrother—now husband—is the CEO of a successful business, after all. However, that thought evaporates quicker than it enters my brain. What could someone like me possibly do in a company like that?

More than ever, I wish I had been able to stay in school. I liked it, honestly. Math was always my favorite. Numbers make sense, no matter what. There's always a solution, and it never changes so long as the variables stay the same. A therapist would probably wave a red flag at that—after all, there wasn't much in my life at that point that made sense, that was dependable and reliable. Not once Mom got sick in my sophomore year.

It's too late for that now. I'm too old to go back, and I would feel ridiculous. Besides, I'm not that girl anymore. I'm somebody else now. I have to be if I want Eric to stay out of my life.

Which is why the best I can hope for is a waitressing job, something basic like that. It's better than nothing, though. It's not like I need much, anyway. I've learned to live simply—I never had a choice.

I'm halfway through applying for one of the positions when there's a knock on the door.

Instantly, my heart leaps into my throat, and my hands shake enough that I have to put the phone down before I drop it on the floor. Is this it? I didn't expect him to announce himself, but then I don't have the first idea what to expect from Lucian. I don't get visitors. I don't have any friends in town, and I like it that way. It's easier to blend in and disappear when you don't have any friends.

Another knock, louder this time, like the person doing it is already running out of patience. I hustle over to the door before anybody can think to kick it open. "Coming!" I hold my breath before turning the knob.

It's not Lucian. It's not anybody I've ever seen before, at least not that I remember. He reminds me of Alexei, though. Big, broad-shouldered, dark hair, dark eyes. "Lucian sent me. You're supposed to come with me."

"Where are we going?"

"You're not supposed to ask questions. You just do what he says. Let's go." He looks around the apartment, and it's pretty clear he doesn't care for what he sees. I know it's not much, but his dismissive expression makes me want to slap him. It's still my home, and it's all I can afford.

I grab my purse and keys, then remember my phone on the sofa. "Hurry up," the man growls, which only makes me want to take my time just to piss him off.

Though word could get back to Lucian, and I don't feel like being punished. Just the thought of it makes me cringe.

There's a black SUV waiting outside, and at least he opens the back door for me and gives me a hand so I can climb up inside. Then he closes the door without a word, sliding in behind the wheel a moment later.

Once again, I can't help but think of myself as a lamb being led to slaughter. "You're not going to tell me anything about where we're going?"

"You'll know when we get there." His eyes are hard when they meet mine in the rearview mirror. "Enough talk." Okay, then. I'm supposed to sit back and let everything be decided for me.

Then again, I know that's what I signed on for when I agree to this. If I could only go back in time and tell Alexei where he could stick his money. It makes me sick to think about him and all his fake helpfulness. His sympathy, all of it a tactic intended to lure me in. I wonder how many other girls he's lured that way and how many more men like him are on Lucian's payroll.

It doesn't matter how many times I tell myself I would've done things differently. The fact is, when Alexei found me, I was literally at the end of my rope. Completely helpless, wondering somewhere in the back of my mind whether it would really be so bad to walk out into traffic.

After a few minutes, we leave the city behind. The houses out here are bigger, well-maintained, sitting in the middle of emerald green lawns. The sort of houses for people whose parents are together, or at least both in the picture. Houses where the parents are healthy, where they don't die from cancer and leave their kids on their own.

Still, I wouldn't imagine Lucian living in one of these houses. I can't imagine him living in a neighborhood at all, really. He doesn't strike me as somebody who would participate in the neighborhood cookout. I can't imagine him bringing a case of beer to his buddy's house to watch the game on a Sunday afternoon.

After several minutes, the houses start moving farther apart. Some of them are behind gates, iron fences. A few of them are so far back and half-hidden by oak trees that I can barely see them from the road. Yes, this strikes me as being more his speed, and sure enough, the driver turns the car toward an open gate and starts rolling down a gravel driveway.

He's taking me to Lucian's house. That's what this has to be about. Unless I'm being loaned out to somebody else, which I guess is possible but isn't anything Lucian warned me about before now. I wish he would have. The sense of my entire life being in his hands is not one I enjoy. I hate not knowing what's going to come next.

But I also have no power in this situation, so all I can do is sit with my hands tightly clenched between my knees, trying to make myself stop shaking.

We pull into a large roundabout in front of a mansion that brings to mind the word *obscene*. It's absolutely massive, with two wings jutting out from a central structure. It's not tacky, though—there are pretty little shrubs and rose bushes in front, carefully trimmed hedges. He does like things a certain way, doesn't he? Everything has to be in its place.

So, where the hell do I fit into all of this?

I don't have to wait long to find out. The driver opens the back door and holds out a hand to me, which I take as a signal to climb out. Once that's done, he leads me through the front door and into an entryway with an enormous iron chandelier in the center. The floors here are marble, polished until they shine, almost slippery as I trot behind the man whose name I never learned. Not that it matters. It's not like I want to see him again.

He leads me up a sweeping staircase that curves in a semicircular shape, then down a long hallway. There are so many rooms. I wonder how many people live here. My entire apartment could fit into the entryway, easy.

At the end of the hall, there's a pair of closed doors set in a wood-paneled wall. It's all very masculine, for sure, but also warm. Almost comforting. I wouldn't have expected that. The few times I've imagined Lucian's life outside of the club, I always pictured him in some cold, soulless penthouse suite.

"Come in," Lucian calls out when the man knocks on the door. Just the sound of his voice brings everything flooding back, our entire last encounter. My confusion, shame, fear.

The driver steps aside to let me into the room, which I can tell at a glance has to be Lucian's bedroom. But it isn't the king-sized, four-poster bed that draws my attention at first.

It's the woman standing next to Lucian at the foot of the bed, silent as I enter.

He never once mentioned anything about adding a woman. There are a lot of things I was expecting, but this wasn't it.

He notices my apprehension, probably because I can't take my eyes off her. She's older than me, probably closer to his age, and not exactly ugly but still not my preference. I guess he decides to take pity on me. "Not to worry," he says, clasping his hands in front of him. "She's a doctor. I brought her over to examine you."

I don't know whether or not I'm supposed to speak, so I decide to keep my thoughts to myself. So he wants me examined. Like he's not sure if I'm healthy, I guess. I would get insulted, but I'm too nervous. Being around Lucian does that to me.

He's probably thinking about what he did, what he made me do. Will he want more of that later? Why else go to the trouble of bringing me out here? He could've had the doctor call me into her office.

"Don't worry," the doctor assures me with a smile. "It won't involve anything you haven't been through before, I'm sure. I need you to undress for me."

I glance toward Lucian. Either he reads my mind, or he never planned on sticking around in the first place. He leaves the room without saying anything else or even looking at me. I can hear his footfalls fading down the hall as I take off my T-shirt.

She's right. This is nothing I haven't been through before. First, she draws a few vials of blood—when I look surprised, she only waves a hand. "To make sure your vitamin levels are where they need to be. You do look a little sallow. Do you get enough sun?"

"Probably not? I don't know."

She nods. "Your D levels could be low. You'd be surprised how many areas of our health are affected by the simplest things." Right, and she's completely bullshitting me right now. I'd never call her on it, like ever. I was taught to respect doctors.

Plus, she's tied in with Lucian, which tells me she's probably not the average doctor. Doctors don't usually make house calls. God knows, I dealt with enough of them when Mom was sick.

After she takes the blood, the doctor has me lie back on the bed. A pap smear? But I'm supposed to believe this is all about my vitamin levels. As always, I close my eyes and wait for it to be over. At least she's quick about it.

She asks me endless questions about my cycle and my last period, and finally, whether I've ever taken birth control.

"No, I never have."

"I'm going to give you a shot today. Depo-Provera. Have you ever heard of it?"

Depo? "Yeah, I've heard of it."

"Lucian requested I give you the shot today, but I have to administer a pregnancy test first." There's no question in her voice, and I know without being told, she won't take no for an answer. Because he won't.

She hands me a cup, and I go to the bathroom to give her a sample. After that, I sit on the bed and watch her work for a few minutes until she finally announces, "You're not pregnant, so I can give you the shot today."

"Terrific." I accept the shot and tell myself at least I know I won't get pregnant.

She gives me the shot in my upper arm and sticks a small band-aid over it. Then packs up her tools. "We're all finished." And that's it. She leaves me alone, naked, except for the sheet she gave me to cover myself with.

What now? Should I get up and dress? Or am I waiting for Lucian? I'm in his bedroom. It makes sense that he'd want something from me.

It's a big room, with what looks like a huge bathroom attached. There's another room next to it that looks like it might be a study or library, and one on the other side of the suite that might be a dressing room. I want to get up and explore—anything to give me a glimpse of who he is—but Lucian's footfalls freeze me in place.

Probably for the best. He wouldn't love it if he found me snooping around.

"You're still undressed." He looks me up and down, buttoning his suit jacket. He even wears suits at home. "Are you feeling unwell?"

"No. I didn't know…" I look down at my lap. He's got to think I'm an idiot.

"Today doesn't count."

"It doesn't?" Dammit. There's a tight feeling in my throat all of a sudden. It's a good thing, isn't it? I should be crying in relief that my thighs won't hurt again so soon.

"No." A smile plays over his lips, but it's over before I get a good look at it. "I won't be fucking you today. Get yourself together and go. The car is waiting."

Dumbfounded, I grab for my clothes and pull them on as he watches. The few glances I throw his way don't tell me anything about what he's thinking. He might as well be wearing a mask.

He doesn't show me to the front door, but I find it on my own.

8

Lucian

I can't remember the last time I spent a whole day away from the club. My business has become my life, and I rarely do things because I want to do them but because I have to do them. So today makes for a refreshing change.

I've been following Rowan around, watching her every move. She's gone to three job interviews, which has me thoroughly surprised. I just transferred her ten grand, and her debt with me is paid. Most women who look like Rowan would go and blow that money on clothes and shoes, then find a rich asshole to keep buying her shit.

The only outfit Rowan bought is the one to wear to the job interviews. This woman has me more intrigued by the minute.

As soon as I got the test results back, letting me know that Rowan is clean, I knew I had to have her today, but I didn't plan on stalking her for so long. I normally like to make it quick. I get bored easily, but there is nothing boring about Rowan. She makes even the most mundane things interesting.

Keeping at least two cars between, I follow the bus she takes to get back to her apartment complex. It's a shit hole, which I was expecting, of course. What I wasn't expecting is how much it would bother me to see the way she lives.

I don't know why I care. All I know is that she doesn't belong here. She should live in a better part of the city, or maybe not in the city at all. A small town with no crime would suit her better.

I'm already parked, the engine shut off, as I watch her get off the bus. Her steps are small but swift, which is probably due to the pencil skirt she's wearing. She looks mighty sexy in it too, like a librarian, schoolteacher, or secretary... my secretary.

My cock is already fighting to get free when I get out of the car and follow her into the building. The front door is unlocked, giving me easy access. Another thing I don't like. She should be protected, and this shithole is anything but.

Shoving that thought away from wherever the fuck it came from. I stay hot on her tail, moving like a predator stalking his prey. Keeping my breathing calm and steady while I step closer with stealth, my heart rate slows down with it.

Digging in her purse, she gets her key out and starts to unlock her door that looks like a gust of wind would knock it down. I take another step toward her, slowly sneaking up behind her.

The lock disengages, and that's when I strike.

I pounce on her so quickly that she doesn't have time to turn around before I shove the door open and push her to the ground inside her apartment. She lands on all fours, giving me a great view of her perfectly shaped ass.

I'm not sure if she doesn't scream because she expects it to be me or is simply shocked. She starts to crawl away as I kick the door shut with my foot and get on top of her.

"None of that," I growl into the shell of her ear while I force her to lay flat on the floor. "I've been watching you all day, shaking your ass at every man in this tight pencil skirt."

"Fuck you!" She hisses, trying her best to buck me off. She even gives me a jab with her elbow but only manages to get me in the arm.

"Don't worry, there will be fucking all right." I chuckle darkly.

Using my body weight, I keep her upper body flat on the ground. Her cheek is firmly pressed against the cheap carpet, and I pry her legs apart with my knees and reach between us with my free hand. Roughly, I shove the skirt up her thighs and grab the flimsy thong covering her pussy. With one harsh pull, the fabric is torn away.

I make quick work of my zipper to free my cock, which is so hard it hurts. Precum is already beading at the tip when I bring it to her cunt. I don't give her time to get wet or adjust. I simply force myself into her tight channel.

She yelps in pain, and her body stiffens beneath me, but I don't stop. This is what I crave. What makes me hard and has my balls tightening, ready for release. I revel in her fight, in her pain. It gives me a kind of power I can only experience in moments like this. Nothing compares.

Mercilessly, I drive into her over and over again. With each stroke, she seems to be growing wetter, but she keeps fighting me until I can feel her thighs quiver and her cunt clamping down on me like she's coming.

"I knew you were a little slut, coming on my cock while I fuck you. You want this. You can act like you don't all you want, but your pussy is wet, creaming over my cock like a whore."

Her body is lax, spent from her release. She is on the floor motionless while I fuck her.

"Time to kick this up a notch. You are enjoying this way too much," I say between clenched teeth while I force myself to pull out of her.

Reaching between us, I dip my index and middle finger into her cunt and drag her wetness up to her asshole.

"Wait," she whimpers, "not there." She starts bucking her hips, and I shove my fingers into her puckered hole, making her yelp. "Fuck!"

"Shut up. I know you want this, slut."

I only pump in and out of her ass a few times before replacing my fingers with my dick.

"Please, no. You're too big. You're gonna tear me."

"Don't worry, my cock is still wet from your soaking pussy. Being a slut and loving my cock is working to your advantage here."

I force the head of my cock past the tight ring of muscle. She squeezes her ass, trying to push me out, but her fight only makes me thrust into her harder. A pained whimper falls from her lips, and my sick and twisted mind feeds on it.

"That's more like it. You will take my cock whenever and however I give it to you. I don't care if you like it or not."

"Please," she whispers. "It's too much."

"If you think this is too much, you are not going to be happy for what I have planned next."

I lift my upper body, grabbing the back of her neck before she can even think about pushing herself up. Using my knees, I push her legs apart even farther so I can get nice and deep. Thrusting forward, I bury myself inside her to the hilt.

A strangled cry falls from her lips, and I loosen my grip on the back of her neck a little, making sure she can breathe.

"You feel me deep inside your ass?" My voice sounds almost distorted as I keep fucking her, my thrusts becoming more furious with each second. "Answer me," I growl.

"Y-yes," she stutters, her voice shaky like she is crying. A normal person would be bothered by her distress. I'm not normal. I'm depraved, twisted, and sick. Her pain is my joy, and her tears make me grin.

After a few more erratic thrusts, the familiar tingle begins in the base of my spine. A moment later, my balls tighten, and I paint her asshole with my cum. My orgasm seems to go on forever, and by the time it stops, I collapse on top of her.

Slowly, I come back down to earth. Sweat is beading on my forehead and dripping onto her shoulder. My chest is heaving, and my heart is slamming against my rib cage, but Rowan is beneath me completely still.

I push myself up and sit back on my knees so I can take a look at her. She still doesn't move. Her legs are spread, giving me the perfect view of my cum dripping down her asshole onto her cunt. Christ, she is perfect.

Tucking away my still sensitive dick, I kneel beside her and roll her over. Her eyes are red from crying, which is a stark contrast to the black streaks of mascara running down the side of her face. The skirt is bunched up around her waist, and her torn-off panties are next to her in shreds.

With glossy eyes, she stares back at me. She doesn't say anything, but there is a question in her eyes, like she wants to know what I'm going to do next.

What am I doing next? I don't fucking know. Simply leaving doesn't feel right.

Still not sure what I'm doing, I slide my arms under her body and pick her up from the floor. Her own arms come to my shoulders, gripping on to me like she fears I'll drop her.

Her apartment is small, and there is only one other door besides the one leading to the hallway so that one has to be her bedroom. I walk inside, confirming it is by the twin-sized bed pushed against the wall.

Gently, I put her down on the mattress before finding my way to the bathroom. I take a washcloth from the cabinet and run hot water over it. By the time I return to the bed, the washcloth has cooled off, and I use it to clean her face. She closes her eyes and actually leans into my touch as I carefully wipe her skin.

Now that I have whipped away the mascara, I notice how her right cheek is an angry red. It was the one I was pressing down into the scratchy carpet, and a ping of guilt hits me. I hate leaving marks. The irony is not lost on me. I don't care if I hurt her, I crave it even, but I don't like there to be marks. It doesn't have anything to do with me not wanting to leave evidence either. I simply don't like marred skin.

When her face is done, I go back to the bathroom and repeat the process with the washcloth. Only this time, I clean between her legs. She winces at my touch but doesn't push me away or tell me to stop. The words, *good girl* are on the tip of my tongue, but I swallow the praise down simply because I enjoy the silence between us. There is no need to explain anything. She knows the kind of monster I am, and I know why she is letting me do this to her.

I help her out of her skirt and blouse before I cover her up with the thin comforter from the foot of her bed. Standing up, I take one last look around the small room, trying to shake how much I hate it that she lives here.

Before I can say something stupid, like you should live with me, I bend down and give her a chaste kiss on her forehead. "Two down, two to go."

9

Rowan

I REALLY WISH I could get a handle on this guy.

And I really wish I understood why I want to get a handle on him at all. This is a temporary arrangement. There doesn't have to be anything more to it than that. Like he said, two down. Two to go. And once that's over, we're finished. There doesn't have to be anything more than that—and there shouldn't be. I have no business in his world, no business with him.

It would be a lot easier to keep that in mind if he wasn't so unpredictable. One minute, he's practically throwing me around, treating me like a thing. An object. Something without any real feelings or thoughts. Like I'm only here for him, for his sake, for his pleasure.

Then he goes and tucks me in with a kiss on my forehead. I've never felt so cared for. My brain is screwing with me, is all. I'm so used to being treated like shit that the slightest little kindness has me all confused.

It would've been easier to wrap my head around last night if he had left me the way I was, on the floor, trying to pull my mind and my body together after what he did. Considering how he treated me, how rough and almost brutal he was, to leave me on the floor without a backward glance would make sense. I could understand that. There wouldn't be any questions this morning.

I can't shake the feeling that there's more to him than what he shows the world. Because for a minute there, he was tender. Sweet and gentle. He treated me like I was more than a few holes for him to fill. Like I mattered.

I'm not an idiot, though. I'm not about to pretend there's more to us than a business arrangement. He's getting what he paid for, and that's it. And if anything, I should be grateful for his consideration. Something tells me that psychopath at the club with the knife wouldn't be so considerate.

Just the thought of that wack job is enough to get me out of bed. A hot shower helps relax muscles I strained during all that fighting last night. It's a good thing this is a temporary arrangement, or else I would be walking around with a heating pad all the time.

Even after that, after I fix a little breakfast and some coffee, I can't get Lucian out of my head. I can't stop looking toward the bedroom, remembering everything.

That's it. I can't stay here all day, going crazy. After washing up the breakfast dishes, I decide to get dressed and go out. It's times like this when I feel the absence of friends. Other girls, especially. Isn't that what we're supposed to do, go shopping together? Granted, I never did like shopping with anybody else. I loved spending time with Eve, but shopping wasn't included in that. Her coming from a rich family was never more apparent than in the times we spent at the mall. When you grow up without any money, every purchase takes consideration. It's a habit I've never been able to break. I doubt I ever will.

Nobody has patience for that kind of thing if they don't understand how it feels. When a shopping trip isn't just something you do for fun on a Saturday afternoon. On top of that, I hate standing around, waiting for other people to make up their minds. It bores me. I would rather shop by myself, even if I can't help but feel a little jealous of the girls walking together in groups at the mall.

The grass is always greener, right?

I can't help but be tempted by the aroma of cinnamon and sugar as I walk past the Cinnabon stand. Maybe I'll stop by later before I leave. It's been ages since I've had one of those completely addictive treats. There are girls who look to be around my age hanging around the coffee stand, where a pair of cute college-age guys are working. They might as well live on another planet. They're so different from me.

What would they think if they knew about the club only a handful of miles from here? I have to bite back a smile. None of them would guess what I've seen, what I've done.

And compared to Lucian, those guys behind the stand might as well be children. Let the other girls have them.

That's a dangerous train of thought. I need to stop thinking that way, or else I might end up regretting it. Lucian's not mine, and he never will be. I don't mean anything to him. As far as I'm concerned, he's given me the funds for this little shopping trip, and he's made it possible for me not to have to take whatever shitty job hires me first. But that's where it ends.

As I walk away from the stand, I can't help but feel like there are eyes on me. It's not one of the guys working there, that's for sure—they're too busy being flirted with, acting like their job is super important and sexy. I look around behind me, over my shoulder, but I can't see anybody out of the ordinary. Just people walking around, a few older folks who look like they're getting their exercise for the day, a pair of women pushing strollers.

For one second, I wonder if Lucian is somewhere around here. If he's watching me again. Following me around, waiting to strike. I wish the idea didn't excite me the way it does. Like I almost hope he's watching from across the food court as I walk through.

Just my imagination running away. After the past week, who could blame it?

I decide to stop in one of the department stores at the far end of the mall. I like the smell of the perfume counter. It reminds me of shopping trips with Mom when I was a little girl. It always felt so fancy and special, walking past the makeup and perfume and jewelry counters. Everything smelled nice. Everything was shiny. So unlike the rest of my life.

I pass the accessories department and eye a couple of cute bags—mine is worn-out, the strap a little tattered after years of use. I make a mental note to stop by on my way out, then continue to the women's section.

It's the weirdest thing. I still can't shake the feeling that somebody's watching. Sure, there are security cameras all over the place, but that's not what I'm feeling. That's not what makes goose bumps rise over my arms. It isn't even the sense of employees watching because they think I'll steal something, which I've experienced before.

"Can I help you?"

I jump about a mile when I hear the girl's voice right next to me. She backs up a step, eyes wide. "Sorry. I didn't mean to scare you."

"It's okay." I laugh, even if my laugh is a little shaky. "I'm jumpy today, I guess."

"Can I help you with anything?" She gestures toward the T-shirts I'm holding. "I can take them to a dressing room if you want. Get it ready for you."

"That would be great, thank you." I hand them to her and decide to look for jeans. I hate shopping for jeans, but I do need at least one new pair. It's just such a hassle with every brand being sized differently. Men have it so much easier when it comes to shopping for clothes.

I decide to grab a couple of pairs in different sizes to see which fits better. I'm about to head for the dressing room when a rack full of pretty dresses catches my eye. They come in different colors—purple, blue, pink, black, and white. I don't have any place special to wear one, but I can't help wondering how one of them would look on me. I can't see spending the money on something I might never wear, though, so it's no use.

This time, when I feel eyes on me, I know it's the girl who's been helping. "That would look great on you." She pulls out a blue dress and holds it up to me, tilting her head to the side. "With your hair and eyes?"

I know it's her job, and I know she's trying to make a commission, but I can't help feeling a little rush of excitement. She's right; it would look great on me. "I guess I'll try it on." I choose one in my size, and she leads me to the dressing room, where she's already left the shirts I picked up earlier.

The dress I'll leave for last, like dessert at the end of a meal. The jeans are all sort of a disappointment—the pair that fits my hips and butt best are a little too loose at the waist. I'll have to find a belt. The T-shirts fit well but are thin, so the lace on my bra shows up. Maybe I'll look for a couple of smooth T-shirt bras before leaving the store. Better yet, I'll stop in at the lingerie store a few doors down.

The bottom line is, I have options, and that feels good. Of course, it's not easy to enjoy shopping when money is tight. But I have a little wiggle room today.

Finally, I try on the dress. It's not even anything that special. The sort of thing I'd wear to a wedding or someplace like that. But it's pretty, with tiny crystals around the low neckline, and the fabric swishes around my knees. It's been a long time since I owned anything nice for no other reason than it makes me feel pretty when I wear it.

I wonder what Lucian would think of it.

I wonder what that says about me.

There's a three-way mirror outside the door, and I decide to take a look. The salesgirl will probably flatter me to hell and back in hopes of making a sale, but that's okay. I haven't been flattered in a long time, either. Sometimes a girl needs that.

My hand is on the knob. I turn it just enough to disengage the lock.

Which is when the door slams open, and I'm shoved against the wall.

It takes a second to understand what's happening since it's all happening so fast. I don't even realize right away who pushed me back into the room.

Until he takes me by the throat and slams me against the wall, harder this time. Very deliberately.

It's the cologne I recognize first, and the scent of it makes my stomach lurch while my brain explodes in panic. I should've known... I should have left the state.

His breath is hot, rancid, wrapping around my face when he leans in close enough for our noses to touch. "You fucking bitch. I knew I'd find you. I always said I'd find you if you ever ran away from me, didn't I?"

I can barely choke out his name. "Eric, please." It's hardly a whisper.

His eyes are so hard, just the way they've been in my nightmares. "Please what, bitch? After making me look for you all this time." His hand tightens around my throat, cutting off my air and making tears spring to my eyes. I hate those tears. I hate them because I know he loves them. He wants to make me cry. But he wants to do a lot worse than that, too.

"I should fucking kill you," he hisses. "For putting me to all this trouble. Making me look like an asshole when you ran away." He raps my head against the wall for emphasis, hard enough to make me see stars.

"Please, don't..." Already the world is starting to go gray around the edges. I claw at his hand, but it's like trying to pry at an iron band. No use. If anything, he squeezes tighter.

"Now, here's what's going to happen." He's eye-to-eye with me, and I can smell liquor on his breath. He's always worse when he's been drinking. "You're coming with me. We're going home. And if you're lucky, you'll be able to leave the house without sunglasses in a couple of weeks. Got it?"

I can't stop the tears now. Everything in me tells me to fight, but it's no use. Not against him. I've learned that lesson the hard way.

Still, the thought of leaving the mall with him and going back to the hell he put me through for so long is so ugly. I'll die there. He'll kill me, or I'll kill myself. Either way, I'm not suffering anymore. I can't. I've been through too much to get away from him.

All of this and so much more flies through my head as he chokes me. "Answer me," he whispers, lifting his chin, baring his teeth. "Answer me now, bitch. Got it?"

I shake my head as much as I can, just an inch or two to either side. "No."

His eyes widen a fraction, and his already red face goes a deeper shade. "What?"

"I said no." And I won't cry anymore. Not because of him, not ever. "I'm not going with you."

I know I'm in trouble even before he smiles. Before the back of his other hand meets the side of my face and sets off an explosion behind my eyes. He holds me up by my throat and hits me again, this time with a fist. Blood rolls down my chin, onto his hand once he's split my lip.

He lets go of me, and I start to slide down the wall, but he picks me up under my arms and steadies me before backhanding me again, and this time, I can't help letting out a cry when my head strikes the wall, and the world goes gray all over again. I end up in a heap on the floor, arms crossed over my head as he winds up for another hit.

"What's happening in here?" It's the salesgirl, trying to open the door. He's standing in front of it, but she manages to open it an inch or two, just enough to see me. "Oh, my god."

"Get the fuck out of here." Eric slams the door shut. "Nosy bitch."

"I'm calling the police!" I can see under the door, and sure enough, she runs off toward the sales floor. I wonder if she realizes he'll kill me before the cops ever show up.

But he doesn't. He settles for kicking me, his foot landing on my hip. "This isn't over, bitch. Watch your back. You can't hide from me."

Then he opens the door and storms out. Only when I can't see him anymore do I let my arms fall from over my head.

The girl comes running back, hands over her mouth. "My god, I'm so sorry. I was on the other side of the floor. I didn't know—"

"It's okay." I can barely speak; both lips are already swollen, bleeding all over the place. Then I realize in horror that I've bled all over the dress, the one I felt so pretty in, the one I was ready to buy even if I didn't have anywhere to wear it.

That's what breaks me. That's what makes my chest tighten, what makes me shake all over.

"It's not okay. You look—"

"I know." I manage to stand with her help, though I have to lean against the wall. Everything's still a little fuzzy.

"I'm going back to the phone to call the cops."

"No, please." I stop short of grabbing her since I don't want to get blood on her. "Don't do that. It'll only make things worse."

There are tears in her eyes, and I realize she can't be any older than me. She might even still be in high school. It's almost enough to make me laugh. I might as well be a walking warning. *Don't let a cute guy trick you into thinking you're less than nothing, or you might end up like me.*

I look down at myself, and for some reason, it's the blood I've dripped onto the dress that makes my eyes well up again. "I'll pay for this."

"Don't worry about it. The store can afford it." She waits outside the dressing room while I put my own clothes on—carefully, so carefully—then ushers me to an employee bathroom where I can clean myself up before stepping outside again. I'm so ashamed, but she insists it's okay. Everything's okay.

Everything's not okay, and it has never been. I only lied to myself enough times that I started to believe the lie.

10

Lucian

I'VE ONLY STAYED AWAY from her for two days, but that's already two days too long.

It's not right. I can't use up my encounters this quickly.

But I can't get anything else done, either, with Rowan running through my mind on an endless loop. The feel of her, the taste of her skin. The sweetness of her sighs, her moans, even when she wants to pretend she's not as turned on as I am.

If anything, breaking her will makes the whole thing hotter. Knowing she can't resist me no matter how she fights it. I know the feeling. I've struggled to resist her since the night I first laid eyes upon her, and I haven't been successful yet.

It might be better to get her out of my system quickly. Once the possibility of being with her is solidly in the past, it will be easier to forget her. The option will no longer be there. The temptation is removed from my subconscious, where it insists on plaguing me.

I summon Rick to my office around mid-afternoon, after waiting as long as humanly possible. He drove Rowan here the day of her examination, so he knows where to find her. "Pick up Rowan and bring her to me." He nods once before turning and leaving the room. Rick's one of my longtime employees, part bodyguard, part driver. He doesn't need to be told more than once to do something, which is one reason he's remained in my employ this long.

I hate having to repeat myself.

Now that I know she's on her way, I can get back to business. The club's books sit in front of me—both of them, the one we use for IRS purposes and the one recording our true numbers. While I trust my accountants, there's nothing like the threat of me reviewing their work to keep them honest.

And the only people who fully trust their accountants are the ones who either end up robbed blind or imprisoned for some stupid mistake. I won't be either of those people. Even making certain all of my employees are generously compensated isn't enough to guard against trouble down the road, and I know it.

Everything looks good from where I'm sitting. The money we take in from big-ticket customers like Glen and his ilk is carefully concealed in membership fees for individuals who don't exist. According to these "official" books, we do brisk business but nothing over the top.

Of course, this isn't my only business. It's one of many, none of which are exactly legal. Neither is paying for sex, but that's what membership fees are for. They're our way around sticky legal problems.

It isn't until I glance at the clock and find a half-hour has passed that I start wondering what's taking Rick so long. I've been to her apartment, and it's not more than ten minutes from the club, even with traffic. She might need time to prepare herself, come to think of it.

And if that's what's taking so long, I can only fantasize about how to punish her once she's with me. Didn't I warn her? She has to be ready for me whenever I want her.

A few minutes pass before my cell rings. It's Rick, and instantly my instincts tell me something's off. He wouldn't call unless there was an emergency or something like that. "What?" I bark into the phone, already put off from having to wait.

"Uh... She's not coming out."

I stand abruptly enough to knock my chair against the credenza behind the desk. "I know you didn't just say that."

"I'm sorry, boss, but she says she can't. She won't even open the door for me."

My free hand clenches into a fist which I slam against the desk. I've waited long enough, and she has the nerve to make me wait longer. I was too easy on her the last time, treating her the way I did. I gave her the idea she has a say in this arrangement.

That will have to be rectified.

"I'll be there in a few minutes. Don't leave her door. If she doesn't want to come out, I'll have to go in—so make sure she stays in there until I show." I end the call, already halfway down the stairs, my irritation rising with every step.

I'm a busy man. She knows this. Does she think this is some sort of game? Was I not clear enough in my instructions? When I want her, she's available to me. It isn't difficult.

Now, I have to take time out of my day to fetch her, like she's a goddamn queen. I wonder if I should've included an engraved invitation for Rick to slide under her door. Perhaps a red carpet for her to walk over on her way to the car.

I fire off the address to another one of my drivers, one I don't trust as much as I do Rick. To think he's not able to get her out of her apartment. I shudder to think what a clusterfuck any of my less-experienced men would turn this into. At least he had the presence of mind to call me rather than trying to force her out and inspiring a neighbor to call the police.

It takes all of eight minutes to reach her building. I spot one of our SUVs out front, telling me Rick stayed put as instructed. No cop cars, so the situation hasn't escalated.

Good thing, since I'd have to take any hush money paid to the cops out of the amount I already paid her. Better yet, I would tack the amount onto her debt, maybe get an extra encounter out of it. The idea doesn't exactly piss me off—in fact, my cock starts to stir at the thought—but I dismiss it as I step onto the sidewalk. It wouldn't be worth the hassle.

Rick stands up straighter when I reach her door, shrugging his thick shoulders in a helpless gesture. "Like I said, she's in there, but she ain't coming out."

Maybe for him. "Thank you, Rick. You can wait out by the car." He's not a smart man, but he knows better than to stick around.

I knock hard on the door. "Rowan. It's Lucian. Open the door."

She must've been waiting on the other side, her voice louder than I expected. "I can't. I'm sorry."

What is it about her voice? Or is it the way she's enunciating? Either way, she sounds slightly off. "Are you ill? What's this about?"

"I just can't, is all. I'm sorry. Give me a few days, please."

She's lisping. I don't know what it means, only that her stubbornness is pissing me off worse than ever. Not to mention the fact that she won't let me see her. Either she's hiding something or…

What if she has a man in there with her?

My blood starts boiling. "Either open the door, or I'll kick it in. Your choice. One… two…"

The lock clicks, but she takes her time to open up. I discover her one bit at a time: bruises around her eyes, a swollen nose, split lips. No wonder she can't speak clearly.

"Who did this to you?" I can barely whisper, but even that makes her flinch. I fully realize how dangerous I sound right now, just as I know there's no hope of making myself sound any other way. Somebody beat the shit out of her.

Somebody beat the shit out of what's mine. Nobody touches what belongs to me.

I step into the apartment rather than have this conversation out in the hall, careful to close the door behind me. "You didn't answer my question."

She lowers her head, letting her hair fall across her battered face. "It's nothing."

I bark out a laugh, making her flinch again. "Don't waste your breath on that shit. This is nothing? You look like somebody used your face for a punching bag. Who did it? Where are they?"

She backs away, eyes as wide as she can get them. He didn't strike her directly in them—it was a man, it had to be—but the swelling of her cheeks gives the illusion of them being swollen. "Please, let it go. I'll be fine in a few days."

"Stop wasting my fucking time, Rowan. I'm going to get answers out of you. Either you can provide them without upsetting me any further or you can continue to test my patience until it shatters. Your choice."

Her chin trembles. Only now do I notice the bruising around her throat, too. I'll kill the motherfucker who did this if it's the last thing I ever do. "It's... he's..." She raises one hand, covering her face, and now her shoulders shake as she begins weeping.

He did this to her, whoever he is.

But I'm not making it any easier. Even now, seeing red, my blood boiling over, I know I'm not helping. So I force myself to draw a deep breath, and when I speak again, my voice is a tad more controlled. "Get some things together. You're coming with me."

"What?" Her head snaps up, her mouth hanging open. I can't help but remember those lips wrapped around my cock. Now they're swollen, ugly. I'll kill him with my bare hands, the son of a bitch.

"You heard me. Get your things, you have two minutes—otherwise, you're coming empty-handed, but you are coming with me. I'll have Rick come back to carry you out if need be." I level a hard gaze at her, arms folding. "Now, Rowan."

It seems I finally got through to her. She disappears into the bedroom, and I hear drawers opening and closing in a flurry of activity. A minute later, she emerges with a duffel bag which I take from her before ushering her out the door.

Once we're in the car, with Rick at the wheel after a few murmured instructions from me, Rowan covers her face again. "I can't stand anybody seeing me like this."

"You have nothing to be ashamed of." I'm gentle but firm, pulling her hands away so I can see her. Now in daylight, it's so much worse.

There are finger marks on her throat. He squeezed her that hard. I've had my hand there and manage to avoid leaving a mark—and I wasn't exactly gentle, either. How vicious is this bastard?

"You don't know how it feels." She sniffles, head hanging low. "I was so afraid you would want to see me before I healed."

"Don't worry about that now. You're safe with me."

She snorts, then looks at me in obvious fear. "Sorry. I believe you. It's just that you don't know him."

My left hand is out of her field of vision, and it tightens into a fist. "Who is he?"

She releases a shuddery breath, obviously arguing with herself. It's either that or the habit of concealing him is so deeply ingrained that she has to fight against the knee-jerk impulse to cover for him. Regardless of why, it takes a moment for her to answer. "My ex-boyfriend. Eric."

Shitty name. "Does this Eric have a last name?"

"Walters." Then she looks at me. "Why?"

"I like to know the full names of the people I want to hurt."

"No, no, you can't do anything." Her eyes well up again. "Not because I'm afraid he'll get hurt. I wish he would. But that'll only make things worse for me in the end."

"Do you believe I have anything to fear from him? Seriously." I glance toward Rick, and she seems to get the hint since her head bobs up and down. "Tell me about Eric. And you. What's the story here?" I want to hear every word, unvarnished. I want her to tell me everything, every last detail.

I want to play it over in my head as I watch him die.

Her hands twist in her lap. She stares down at them while speaking. "He's the reason you couldn't find anything about me online. Remember? When I first came to the club?"

That explains it. I'd almost forgotten. "So your name isn't Rowan?"

"No, it is, but I closed out all of my online accounts before I left him. I saved up every penny I could for months and finally ran when I couldn't take it anymore. He was out with his friends that night—I knew when he'd come home since he always showed up an hour or so after the bars closed. I can't tell you how many times I sat up in bed, dreading the sound of him coming in. I got a fake driver's license with a fake address, so there's no true record of me in the DMV database anymore. I didn't tell anybody—not like I have any friends to tell, anyway. He made sure of that. He made sure of a lot of things."

"But he found you."

She nods slowly. "I don't know how. He didn't say. He followed me to the mall and did this to me when I was in a dressing room." Her voice cracks, and she wipes away a tear. "He's crazy. He's never gone that far before. Hitting me in public? He would never have done that."

Because she's no longer his. She ventured out on her own, away from him, and it enraged him worse than ever. I can almost imagine the level of rage that would drive a man to do something like what he did to her.

But that's as far as it goes. Only the lowest man beats a woman, especially one as small and defenseless as Rowan. I've witnessed enough harm done in the name of satisfying a kink to know there are situations in which one or both parties might emerge wounded, hurt.

This isn't one of those situations. Nobody paid her to let them beat her. There was no consent here—only pain and fear. And a cowardly little piece of shit who probably considers himself a man.

"He wanted me to go with him. He actually thought I would leave the store with him." She laughs humorlessly. "I couldn't. I knew he'd kill me if I went—maybe not right away, but eventually. It's why I left in the first place. I knew it would never get better because he'll never get better. Can you believe I used to think he would?" She says in disbelief.

Yes, she would've done better to wait for Santa Claus to slide down the chimney. People like him never change. "Thank you for telling me about him. I'm sure that couldn't have been easy." Considering the blinding rage now consuming me, I think I sound downright gentle. It's enough for her shoulders to fall slightly as if the tension is finally draining away.

She looks out the window. "Are we going to your house now?"

"Yes. You'll be safe there. If he found you at the mall, no telling how long he's been following you. There's no way he'll know to look for you anywhere near me." But I know him, or I will once my guys finish looking for him. Eric Walters. He doesn't know it, but his days are numbered.

Once we're at the house, I hand her bag over to Rick and lead her upstairs and down the hall. "There's plenty of room here, as you know."

"Your bedroom?" She steps into the suite in which her examination took place, her head on a swivel as she looks around.

"This isn't my bedroom. Mine is at the other end of the hall." I extend an arm in that direction. "You have full use of the suite, along with anything else in the house, except for my suite of rooms. They're off-limits. Understood?"

She nods, swallowing—and wincing when she does. I make a note to request a pot of tea for her, something to ease the pain. "Come on. I'll run you a bath. Soaking for a while will help relax you." I don't wait for her to accept, going straight to the bathroom and turning on the faucet. Soon steam rises up in a cloud. Rowan lingers in the doorway, watching me with obvious anxiety.

"What?" I straighten up, looking around the room. "Is there something wrong here? Is there anything missing?"

She shakes her head. "No. It's beautiful here. But I know you're a busy man. You must have a million more important things to think about."

The girl isn't wrong. There are a million things in need of my attention. Damned if I can think of a single one that doesn't directly involve her. "Don't worry about that. Just do as I say, and you'll be fine. Enjoy your bath." I leave her alone then, and not a moment too soon. I don't know how much longer I could've maintained a neutral expression, something that wouldn't scare her worse than she's already been scared.

Rick's waiting for me in the hall, and the look we exchange tells me he knows what's coming. "Eric Walters," I snarl. "Find that bastard for me."

He nods, his lip curling in disgust. "Gladly."

11

Rowan

This isn't how I saw my day turning out; that much is for sure.

Soaking in this enormous tub which is more like a swimming pool. I could invite five people to join me and still have plenty of room to stretch out. It took a minute, but I figured out how to turn on the jets, and they've been working magic on my sore muscles.

Not that I've been doing a lot of heavy lifting in the past couple of days or anything like that. This is the sort of soreness that happens when a person has been tense for too long. And that's how I've been since my trip to the mall, where I left empty-handed—one big ball of tension. Always waiting for the other shoe to drop, for Eric to barge through the door.

Now, I don't have to worry about that. I can close my eyes and disconnect from everything for a little while.

Isn't it strange, relying on Lucian for protection? He's the sort of guy a girl needs protection from, right? But here I am, soaking in his tub. Able to breathe, finally.

Eric would have to be the world's biggest idiot to follow me here, even if he saw me leaving the apartment with Lucian and his driver.

I almost wish he would. For once, he would get what's coming to him.

If my lips didn't hurt so bad, I would smile. It's better to keep them as still as I can, not to smile or even open my mouth too wide. They'll never heal otherwise. One of the many lessons Eric taught me over the years. A few days shy of two years, in fact. Looking back, I can't figure out why I stayed as long as I did.

That's easy to think, looking back. When a girl is in the middle of hell with no visible way out, it's not so easy to sit on a high horse and pass judgment. The fact is, all I could do then was survive. Which meant being on my best behavior as much as possible, making sure I did nothing to upset him. I walked on eggshells for those two years.

You're walking on eggshells here, too.

I'm not a huge fan of the voice in my head right now. I don't need to be reminded that I have no idea what any of this means. What I now owe Lucian. No way is any of this being offered for free. Men like him don't hand out favors for nothing. He'll find a way to make me pay him back.

I guess all I can do is hope his repayment method is less painful than what I would've dealt with from Eric.

The bath is a nice start, anyway. It gives me hope. Maybe this won't be so bad. Maybe I'll actually be able to sleep tonight, now that I won't have to be worried about my door getting kicked in.

Though that doesn't mean I can be completely relaxed. I need to remember who I'm with. The man is dangerous—there was a minute in the apartment when I was afraid he might start throwing things, or worse. I've seen that sort of rage cross a man's face before. I've seen it up close and personal, and not all that long ago.

In a way, Lucian reminds me of Eric. He's polished and sophisticated and definitely sexier than Eric could ever hope to be on his best day. But he's also brutal. He's done brutal things to me, even if all of it was sort of fake. Like the way he told me to fight back because he wanted me to.

He's just as dark inside as Eric is. The difference between them is Lucian has found a way to let that side of himself out. He has fun with it, even if his idea of fun is pretty dark and twisted. In the end, he wants to feel like he controls me or any woman he's with.

And when it comes right down to it, that's how Eric is, too. They're like two sides of the same coin.

That's what's on my mind when the bathroom door opens and Lucian enters the room. He didn't knock or anything. He probably figures that's his right since this is his house. Either way, I'm not about to argue with him.

He checks his watch. "You've been in here for forty-five minutes."

"I have?" When I look at my fingers, they tell the story. My skin is beyond pruney. "I guess I lost track of time."

"You'll boil yourself alive before long." He takes a pair of towels from a stack beside the tub, and I take that as a hint. I've soaked long enough. It's okay. I can't imagine spending more time in here anyway.

He helps me out of the tub, taking me by the arms like he's afraid I'll slip and fall. That's not the most surprising thing, though. It's when he shakes out one of the towels and starts drying me off. He doesn't say a word, doesn't ask if I want help.

He's not gentle about it, either. In fact, he's a little rougher than he needs to be. I find myself wincing as he rubs my skin, but I hold my tongue for fear of what might happen if I complain.

He's angry, obviously, just the way he was in the car. If there's one thing I know, it's not to push someone's buttons when they're already angry. Wasn't I just comparing him to Eric a few minutes ago?

I don't know how much more of this I can take. Living in fear. Just because Lucian lives in a mansion and I'll be comfortable here doesn't mean the fear will go anywhere. A gilded cage is still a cage.

My heart is racing when he turns me around to dry off my front. He won't look me in the eye—I'm not sure how I feel about that, whether it's a good thing or not. The tightness of his jaw worries me, for sure. He looks like he's ready to kill somebody.

He wanted me today, and it's obvious I'm not available for him. Not in that way. I honestly can't imagine even pretending to be forced into fucking him. I'm too raw, and I might be for a while.

What if he decides to take the money back? I haven't spent very much of it—only the one outfit for the interviews. That doesn't matter, though, because I can't give it back. It would leave me with nothing, and I'd be at square one all over again.

After all this? No, I can't do that. I can't go back to the way things were before, not after days spent dreaming of how much easier life will be now that I know I have a nest egg in case everything goes to shit.

I'm starting to feel a little woozy, and it's getting hard to breathe. I need some fresh air. The room is too steamy, and I can't pull in a decent breath.

"Rowan?" Now Lucian is looking at me, studying me with a scowl twisting his usually handsome features. "What's wrong with you?"

Everything. That's what I want to say because that's the answer. Everything is wrong with me. As wrong as it can be. Just when I think I'm getting ahead. Just when I think things are finally starting to go my way, something always happens. Something gets fucked up. It's not even my fault this time—I was as careful as I could be, but Eric found me anyway.

And now Lucian is mad at me. He's going to take away the money, and I won't even be able to afford my crappy little apartment anymore. What am I going to do? How am I supposed to make it through this?

He catches me before I hit the floor. My legs are shaky, my knees weak. He sits me on the edge of the tub, then crouches in front of me. "Breathe. That's all you have to do right now. Breathe."

But I can't, and I can't tell him I can't. All I can do is shake my head.

He wraps a towel around me, lifts me in his arms, and carries me into the bedroom. In the back of my mind, fear takes hold. So he does want sex. I should've known. My panic only rises, and all I can do is breathe in tiny little gasps.

He sets me down, then opens the nearest window. A rush of cool air flows toward me, making goose bumps rise on my damp skin. But it's nice. Refreshing.

"All you have to do is breathe. That's all you need to do right now. In and out, slowly." He stands in front of me, arms folded, and I can't help but think I'm only pissing him off more than ever. He so impatient, and I know his time is valuable. I've already wasted enough of it today.

Dear god. What am I supposed to do? How do I get out of this?

"Are you in pain?" I shake my head because I'm not. "Good. Anything else, we can deal with."

That's what he thinks. He's not in my place. Wondering what the hell is going on through the head of the person in front of him. What the rest of his life is going to look like. Whether he's going to be out on the street.

"Lie down. Relax." He walks around the bed while I do as he says, gingerly stretching out while still wrapped in the towel. It's like lying on a cloud, absolutely luxurious, even nicer than the soak in the tub. If I had a bed like this, I would never leave it.

I can't help but flinch at his touch. He climbed into the bed without me noticing, and he isn't wearing his suit jacket anymore. He slides one arm under me, draping the other over the top of me, and pulls me a little closer.

All I do is wait. It's inevitable; his touch will change. His arms will tighten, and maybe he'll clamp a hand over my mouth. For all I know, this is turning him on, knowing how defenseless I feel. How scared I am. I'm not putting it on this time, either. This isn't for show. I'm genuinely scared out of my mind.

"Relax. I'm not going to bite you." Is that humor in his voice? I can't tell. If it is, he's laughing at me, but I don't care. It's better than him being so angry.

"Sorry. I'm just upset."

"You don't have to apologize for being upset. You've been through a lot. I have to admit, I had forgotten about you being so hard to find online. Now that you've explained the situation, I wonder how I didn't put it together for myself."

Why would he think that much about me in the first place? I want to ask, but I don't dare. I can't shake the feeling of there being an invisible line between us, one I don't dare cross. But that's the thing about invisible lines: if they're invisible, you don't know where they are or when you've crossed them.

Not until it's too late.

"All you have to do now is rest. You have nothing to be afraid of here. Tell me you understand that."

Sure, but it will be a lie. Just about everything about Lucian scares me —most especially the fact that he was the first person I thought of when I got home after the mall. Wondering if I could or should reach out to him. Whether it would be okay to ask him for help — and whether I could afford the payment in return. That was what stopped me, knowing he doesn't do anything for free. I didn't want to end up indebted to him even further since God knows what I'd have to do to pay it off.

He expects me to answer, so I do. "I understand."

"But you took your time answering."

I close my eyes, wincing, glad that my back is to him so he can't see my face. "When you've been through what I have, it's not easy to trust. I'm sorry, but that's the truth."

He's quiet for a few seconds, long enough that I can't help but wonder if I've offended him. Finally, he sighs in my ear. "Yes, I suppose it would be difficult." Is it just me, or do his arms tighten a little bit when he says it? Almost like he's hugging me.

It's dangerous, thinking that way, but it also makes me feel good. If I can trick myself into thinking this is all for my benefit, that he's doing this for me as opposed to protecting an investment or something like that, I can finally and fully relax. I sink deeper into the bed, into the pillows under my head. I can feel safe with his arms around me. Like nothing in the world will touch me so long as I'm with him.

"There's something about me I want to make clear, here and now. No matter what I do to you or to any other woman in the service of my needs, I detest anyone who takes their frustrations and feelings of inadequacy out on a weaker person. They're the worst kind of coward, and there's no place for them in society. I hate thinking of you suffering at the hands of someone like that. And I wish I had known he might one day be a problem, so I could've helped you avoid him."

It takes a minute for what he's saying to sink into my brain. "You would've done that? Help me, I mean?"

"I don't say things I don't mean, Rowan. Yes, I would've done my best to see to it you were safe, away from him. While I understand your reticence, I hope you understand now that it's best to be honest with me."

"But I didn't know." To be honest, I still don't. I can't figure him out. One second, he looks like he's ready to kill somebody, and the next, he's practically rocking me to sleep in his arms.

"Now you do. You need something, you tell me so."

"Okay. I will."

"Now try to get some sleep. You're overtired, distraught. Some rest will help. And when you wake up, there's plenty to eat and drink in the kitchen. I want you to take care of yourself."

"I will." And as I close my eyes, if only for his sake, I try to convince myself he's being sincere. That he only wants to help me out. I wish I could believe him, that's all. I wish I could shake the idea of there being strings attached somehow. Maybe I'm not being fair to him, but screw fair. Life hasn't exactly been fair to me, either.

After a while, his arms loosen, and he slides away from me. I start a little but settle back down, my eyes still closed. Let him think I'm asleep. He walks slowly and quietly from the room and closes the door without hardly making a sound, leaving me alone.

I wish I could understand him.

12

Lucian

It wasn't easy to leave her, knowing how distressed she is. I did what I could to see to her comfort before I left, at least. Knowing she's here rather than out in the world somewhere that piece of shit could find her brings me a measure of peace.

A small measure. Otherwise, my insides are churning the way they've done since I first set eyes on her this afternoon. So wounded, frightened. Thinking a locked door would protect her from her ex. If he could follow her to the mall, he must know where she lives by now.

I wonder what's kept him from charging into her apartment—then, I admit there's nothing to wonder about. I can't pretend I've never done my share of stalking. For fuck's sake, I stalked Rowan only days ago.

I didn't want to harm her, though. That's the difference between us—one of many.

He loved the idea of hurting her, breaking her body, and twisting her mind. Living in her head. Knowing every time she looked in the mirror or touched her face, she'd think of him. Picture him looming over her. He's drawing out the tension—or thinks he is.

Little does he know.

Alexei texts me a couple of hours after I return to the club. *On the way. Everything set.* I know what that means, and I can't help smiling. This day took an interesting turn, but it's about to end pleasurably. At least, for me.

Getting up, I walk over to the bar cart to pour myself a drink, savoring it in the minutes before Alexei and Rick return with their prize. For someone with a penchant for beating and humiliating women, Eric ought to practice more care when it comes to covering his tracks. Who knows when an enraged parent or sibling will come looking for revenge.

Though he would be careful about that, wouldn't he? He would prey on women like Rowan, the ones with no family or friends. The ones who've been alienated from the world for one reason or another. A part of me knows that I've done the same, preying on women who are down and need money, but at least I don't enjoy their misery.

She deserves better than that and a hell of a lot better than him. I might be a hypocrite, but I can't help it when it comes to Rowan. She is mine.

Mine. He touched what's mine. I take another sip of my whiskey and will myself to be calm. The son of a bitch doesn't deserve for this to end quickly. I want to take it slow with him. I want to make sure to create plenty of memories worth savoring. By the time it's finished, he'll regret ever drawing his first breath.

I'm seated behind my desk again by the time Alexei's knock rings out. I open the door using the remote, then remind myself to take a deep breath. To calm down and enjoy this.

A man who can only be Eric stumbles into the room with Alexei on one side, Rick on the other. "What's this all about?" He pulls his arms away from the guys, making sure to snarl at both of them. The big man, so strong, so frightening.

He doesn't frighten me. He didn't before I laid eyes on him, and he certainly doesn't now. A pretty boy? I'm almost disappointed in Rowan for falling for somebody like him. All surface flash—blond hair, blue eyes, a square jaw. White teeth, which he bares in a snarl. "Well? Who are you? What's going on? Why did these two grab me when I was getting in my car?"

I lean back in my chair, satisfied to stare at him silently for a while. How many times did he drive those fists into her face, her body? How many times did he wrap his hands around her throat and squeeze until she was at the edge of consciousness?

He snaps his fingers. "Hello? Are you deaf or something? You send your goons after me but won't bother telling me why?"

Finally, I sigh. "Let me ask you a question, Eric Walters. Why do you think you're here?"

It's delicious, the flash of fear in his eyes when I call him by his full name. He's asking himself how I could possibly know who he is.

He lowers his brow, his expression hardening. "I don't have the first fucking clue, which is why I asked you. Why did you have them bring me here?"

"I've heard a lot about you."

"About me?" He points at himself and smiles like this is all a big misunderstanding. "Sorry, pal, but you got the wrong guy. I've never laid eyes on you in my life."

"I know all about you, just the same. I know you came to town for a particular purpose."

He raises an eyebrow. "Oh, yeah? And what purpose is that?" The fact that he hasn't yet dropped this act of false bravado is partly admirable, partly pitiable.

"Stop." I hold up a hand, shaking my head. "You're making a fool out of yourself. Stop pretending. We both know you came here for her."

It's incredible, really. Watching him shift the way he does until he might as well be a different person. "That's what this is about?" he growls. "What, did she hire you to take care of me? You don't know the first thing about her."

"Don't I?" I tent my fingers beneath my chin. "Please, enlighten me."

"For one thing, she ran off on me. She stole my money, and she ran."

I know this is a lie, but I pretend to buy into it. "I can imagine. It looks like you resorted to going through clothing donation boxes to put your outfit together."

He looks down at himself, scowling. "Okay, big joke. Whatever. You don't know me, and you don't know what I went through with that girl. Here I was, thinking she might be dead or something."

"Which is it? Did you come after her because she stole from you, or because you wanted to be sure she wasn't dead or something?"

"Both. And I don't have to explain myself to you." He straightens out his jacket, which wasn't very rumpled to begin with. "Now, if you don't mind, I'm leaving." He turns toward the door, only to find my guys blocking the way.

"I'm afraid it's not that easy. I can't let you walk out of here."

"And why not?" He glares at me over his shoulder. "I don't owe you anything. And whatever she told you, it's probably all a bunch of lies anyway. You can't trust a person like that."

"Right, because she did steal from you."

"Exactly! I'm out with my buddies. I come home, and she's gone."

"With your money."

"Yes, for God's sake!"

I really should stop toying with him, but it's too much fun. And a man like me doesn't get a lot of fun in his life. "I can imagine why you would be upset and why you might feel compelled to go after somebody like that. You would at least want to get the last word, to take back some of what was stolen from you."

"You're fucking right."

"Now, tell me. Where does stalking her, following her into a dressing room, and beating the shit out of her fit into that?"

"Hold on a second—"

I stand, cutting him off. "Enough with your lies. I'm tired of hearing them. In fact, I'm tired of hearing your voice." I glance toward Rick, who takes this as a signal to grab Eric from behind, taking him by the arms. Before he has time to struggle, Alexei shoves a wadded-up rag into his mouth.

"That's better." I smile at him, at the naked fear in his eyes. And at the sweat now rolling down the sides of his face. It's so easy to break a coward, especially one who tries to put on a good show the way this one does. All an act. "Now, I can tell you why you're here."

I walk in a slow circle around him, taking my time. Savoring every one of his short, panicked breaths. "You put your hands on Rowan. You hurt her, badly. And from the way she describes it, that wasn't the first time—far from it, in fact. Even if she did steal from you, which I highly doubt, she only took what she deserved after what you put her through."

I come to a stop in front of him. I smell his sweat now, acrid. The way a man sweats when he's truly terrified. "That wasn't enough for you, though. You had to threaten and humiliate her—and in public, at that. Can you imagine what that was like? Bloodied with bruises forming. Having to drag herself out of the dressing room, through the store? Having to get herself home somehow when her face probably felt like somebody had taken a hammer to it? Have you ever had to do that?"

I shake my head. "Of course not. Because you've never fought anyone who had a chance of beating you. You choose the smaller ones, the weaker ones. Women, naturally. But I would bet you were a bully in school, too. A big-mouth asshole who made it his life's work to humiliate the smaller kids. You're all the same, you cowardly piece of shit."

I pause, taking a breath, watching his every movement. "Tonight, that changes. You'll understand how it feels to face someone bigger than you. I've been looking forward to this for hours." I turn back to my desk and finish what little is left of my drink. I held myself to one this evening since I don't want to dull my senses.

Meanwhile, Eric struggles. Everybody but him knows it's a waste of energy, but I have to give him credit for trying. I wouldn't expect him to give up and take it.

The thing about running a business like mine is how no one seems to notice or mind when a man is half-dragged down a hallway with a gag in his mouth. Compared to some of the kinkier activities even in

Heaven, that's a typical Tuesday night. The fun continues on both sides of the hallway as I follow Eric and the guys to the stairs leading straight down to Hell.

Tonight, Hell is going to live up to its name for Eric.

We end up in one of the empty rooms near the end of the hall. The black walls and ceiling are the same as every room on this level. What sets this room apart is its lack of toys, tools, and gadgets. There's only a single wooden chair in the corner closest to the door and a bare bulb hanging from the center of the ceiling.

Alexei and Rick toss Eric into the center of the room, then leave us alone. Eric tears the gag free and throws it on the floor before snarling at me. "So that's what this is about? You bring me down to the basement to fight me? What, you think you're her hero or something?"

"I'm nobody's hero." I take my time, slowly removing my jacket, folding it down the middle, and draping it over the back of the chair.

"So, what are you, then? Did she pay you?"

I snort while unfastening my cuff links. "No."

"What is it, then?"

"Let's say I believe in justice." I roll up my sleeves with a smile. "And justice is going to be served tonight."

There's naked fear in his eyes when they dart over me, sizing me up. "You think you'll get justice tonight? I don't know, buddy. I've got maybe twenty pounds on you."

I tilt my head to the side, frowning. "Me? You think I'll be the one you face tonight? I'm only getting comfortable before I settle in for the show." I go to the door and tap my knuckles to it. "No, Eric. I was going to kill you myself—I was looking forward to it, honestly."

The door begins to open, and I can't hold back a smile. "Then I came up with an idea that's even more fun."

And oh, it is. The pleasure of watching his face go slack at the sight of the men entering the room is exquisite. There is probably six hundred pounds of muscle between them, a pair of twins who went through some extremely fucked up shit in their youth and have spent a lot of time in prison. Just like anybody else, they sometimes need to work out their pent-up aggression.

I do like giving people an outlet for their aggression.

"Oh, yeah." Luke pounds his fist into the other palm. "Yeah, he'll be fun."

Mark nods, chuckling as he strokes his bushy beard. "Thumb wrestle to see who gets him first."

Eric backs away, gasping for air, holding his hands up. "No, no, no. You don't have to do this."

Fucking coward. I take a seat on the chair, nodding to the twins. "Whenever you're ready."

Luke's impatient, taking the first swing at Eric's midsection, causing him to double over, clutching his stomach, and Mark drives a knee into his nose. The sound of breaking bones makes me smile.

Mark pulls off Eric's jacket, then holds his arms behind him while Luke takes another swing, this time aiming for the ribs. "How does that feel?" I ask, raising my voice over Eric's broken sobbing. "Being hit by somebody bigger than you. Being at their mercy. Not being able to defend yourself. I want you to think about that."

Mark throws Eric at the wall, where Luke grabs him and tears his shirt open before tossing the scraps to the floor. "It's gonna be so fun fucking your ass," Mark says with a laugh.

When Eric's head snaps up, eyes wide and wild, the brothers laugh.

"Don't forget the foreplay, boys," I remind them. "Make sure he's nice and loosened up before you take that virgin ass."

Eric slumps to the floor, the bottom half of his face now covered in blood. The sense of satisfaction this brings me is impossible to describe. I can only feel it, and it feels like warm honey pouring over me. He'll pay for every time he ever hurt her. Every time he ever put a hand on her, every time he ever fucked her. The balance will be paid in full tonight.

"Please." His eyes pierce me, pleading, sparkling with tears that roll down his cheeks and cut through the blood. "Please, no."

"Don't worry. You won't remember a thing when it's over." My smile widens when understanding dawns. When he realizes he won't leave this room alive.

I'm so glad I didn't drink too much. I want to be able to savor every moment with a clear head. I lean back in my chair and watch as the twins strip Eric of his clothing. Luke shoves him to the floor, and Mark disappears from the room to get some toys.

"I'm sorry, please don't do this. I'll forget she ever existed. I'll leave." His lies only infuriate me more. It doesn't matter if he leaves Rowan alone because there will always be someone else. A new girl will come along, and he will do the same to her. Killing this piece of shit will be doing a favor for the rest of the world.

"It's not about leaving her alone. We're way past that; you're going to pay the price for your wrongdoings."

Mark returns to the room, closing the door behind him. I can make out the huge dildo in his hand as he steps into the light. It's thick, and Eric's going to feel every raw inch of it as Mark shoves it into his ass without an ounce of lube.

"Please, I'm begging you." Eric's eyes bleed into mine, his own fears reflecting back at me. I feed off that fear, feasting on it like it's my last meal.

"I'm sure she begged you to stop as well." I pause for a moment, letting my words sink in. "Carry on, Mark."

Mark smiles gleefully as Luke pins Eric to the floor, securing his hands behind his back. He struggles but doesn't get far. Mark pulls him back, sits on his legs, spreads his ass cheeks, and slams the dildo between them. A scream, so deep and painful, pierces the air, and I smile, enjoying his screams and pleas for us to stop as Mark fucks his ass with the dildo until he starts bleeding.

After that, Luke cuts his cock off, and the puddle of blood surrounding him grows bigger. By the end of the night, I'm feeling a little lighter. Rowan deserved to be here to see this fucker get ass raped, but it's best she isn't. I'm not sure she would follow through with the rest of our deal if she did.

13

Rowan

WHAT WAS I just saying to myself last week about a gilded cage?

I can hardly believe it's been a week, but the calendar doesn't lie. I've lived in Lucian's house for seven days. I've wandered through this palace of a house, smack dab in the lap of luxury. And I still don't know why I'm still here.

It'd be helpful if I could ask him about it, but that would involve telepathy. I haven't seen him since that first day in bed. If I had known he would cut himself off from me for a week, I would've said something before he left me alone in bed. I might've thanked him or something like that.

How was I supposed to know he would disappear?

No, disappear isn't quite the right word. He's still very much here sometimes. I've heard his shoes hitting the hardwood floor in the hallway more than once. I even saw him go into his room—at least, I saw the back of him a split second before he closed the door and shut me out. So I know he's been here.

It's just that I haven't seen him face-to-face. And I don't know whether it's been deliberate on his part or what. Is he going out of his way to avoid me?

It's so stupid, even wondering about things like this. I'm sure he doesn't waste a second thinking about me—if anything, it probably makes him feel better, more secure, knowing I'm right here whenever he wants me. Whenever he gets that itch that only I can scratch. Otherwise? I might as well be nobody. Why would he think about me even a second longer than he had to?

But I'm not a pet. I'm not something for him to own, to visit when he feels like it, and leave for someone else to take care of when he gets bored with me.

I would tell him this, too, if he would show his face. I really would. At least, that's what I tell myself as I sit alone for hours on end. One day bleeding into another, and I'm still no closer to knowing when the hell I can go home. Or if he ever intends on letting me go home at all.

At least there are plenty of books to read, and he already told me I have the run of the house except for his room, so I've spent some time catching up on movies and TV shows I either didn't have time to watch before or couldn't afford the subscription for. He has everything, of course, all the channels, all of the streaming services. I have the entire world at my fingertips.

I don't have anybody else to talk to. I don't have him. I don't even have the household staff, though they're kind and thoughtful. Greta, the cook, is especially sweet. She never asks questions about why I'm here or who I am. There's no judgment, either. She asks if I'm hungry and what I like to eat, and the next thing I know, there's an entire meal in front of me.

I can't help but remember watching *Beauty and the Beast* with Mom when I was little. Lucian isn't a beast—not physically, anyway—and I've never considered myself a beauty people randomly break out into song over. But this is a lot like that situation, where Belle was locked away in the Beast's castle. She could do anything she wanted except leave. She could have everything she needed as long as she obeyed the rules.

Only this is no fairy tale.

It might be easier to handle if I knew when I could leave. If there was something on the horizon to look forward to.

It's enough to make me laugh when I take walks around the grounds, always aware of being watched. There are guards all over the place—some of them easily visible, some not so much. I can't make a move without one of them observing it. Sometimes I want to do something crazy, like jump in the pool or uproot one of the plants, just to see what they would do. Let them earn their money.

Nobody in her right mind would want to leave this place. I know that. And I don't want to leave, not exactly. If I could stay here with the promise that things would make sense and be less awkward, I would happily say yes. If I could come and go as I please, and if I didn't feel so much like I'm alone on a desert island.

Because Greta is the only person who talks to me. I've said hi to many of the men I've come across, but all of them look either annoyed with me or like they're afraid to say anything back. What? Did Lucian warn them not to talk to me? What could be so bad about that? If he's going to leave me here, essentially stranded, I should at least be able to have a conversation with somebody.

One thing hasn't changed: I still make sure every day to be ready for him if he wants me. Not that it's any huge hardship or anything. I like soaking in the tub, and everything I need is right there in the vanity.

That's one thing I would like to ask him about. How did he know what to have here for me? All of the makeup I wear—my shade of foundation, the lip gloss I use—all of it is in the vanity drawers. And they were all brand-new, like they just came from the store, wrapped in plastic or sealed shut.

Either he's a mind reader, or he had somebody break into my apartment and go through all of my things so they would know what to buy for me.

The idea makes my stomach churn. The thought of some random strangers going through my things. No, I don't have a lot, but that's not the point. What's mine is mine.

I don't know who Lucian thinks granted him access to my entire life, but I would like to revoke it if possible.

It's a little late for that, isn't it?

Right away, I feel guilty for even thinking along these lines. I get out of the tub and dry off on one of the thick, insanely soft towels. As I step onto the heated floor and sit down in front of the vanity chockfull of my favorite brands. I'm being ungrateful, aren't I? After all, I could never imagine living in a place like this on my own. I should try to make the best of it and enjoy it as much as I can, right? Without all this thinking and uncertainty.

I examine my face, and I'm relieved to see the swelling has completely gone down. Greta didn't ask any questions about that either. Thank god. No way would I have been able to get through it without breaking down. I've been carefully applying my brand-new makeup to the bruises, and it's been helpful. I don't have to flinch away in disgust whenever I catch sight of myself in a mirror.

My clothes are the right sizes, too. That's another clue that tells me somebody went through what I left in the apartment. The day after I came here, I woke up to a closet and dresser full of clothes. Not just any clothes, either. The sort of things I couldn't imagine ever buying for myself, with labels that made my eyes bulge when I read them.

He does realize I'm not used to this kind of thing, right? He didn't need to spend all this money to keep me satisfied. I guess for a man like him, this is a drop in the bucket.

And for all I know, I'm not the only girl he's ever done this for. It does seem like he had a whole little system in place, come to think of it. Like in no time at all, he got me settled into his house. No questions, no confusion. One minute the closet was empty, and the next, it was full of clothes. Whoever put my things away didn't even wake me up. Yet another unnerving thought. Somebody creeping around while I was asleep.

I would ask Lucian about this, too, if he would talk to me. I should make a list.

I slide into a pair of ankle boots to complete my outfit—jeans and a tunic, both of them fit like they were made for me, which is amazing considering the difficulty I had finding jeans at the store—and then decide to take a walk. It's the only thing I can do besides sitting around the house, and at least the grounds are pretty.

Today I take a walk through the garden, where roses like the ones blooming out front grow in a dazzling range of colors. I had never seen apricot roses before now, and they're so perfect. I almost want to take one and bring it inside, but I know that would ruin it. It's better to let it grow on its own and admire it.

It sort of seems like a waste, I muse as I walk down the carefully maintained paths. Lucian is never around to enjoy any of this, so why go to all the trouble of paying somebody to maintain the grounds so meticulously? As far as I know, he doesn't throw parties here. No houseguests besides me. Even having staff on hand at all times seems pointless when there's no one to serve.

I ask Greta about that when I go inside for breakfast. "It's better not to ask questions," she informs me with a motherly smile. "The boss has his ways, and he's very particular about how he likes things to be done."

"I figured that out on my own."

"If he's happy, that's enough for me. I do my work, which I know he appreciates, and I'm left to my own devices. In the grand scheme of things, it's a very comfortable situation." She pours eggs into a pan and scrambles them for me just the way I like them, while a slice of wheat bread browns up in the toaster.

I know she lives somewhere on the grounds, but not here in the house. I've noticed a couple of small cottages at the far end, but I've never gone back there. That would take me beyond what can easily be seen from the upstairs windows, and I don't like the idea of having somebody following me around on foot.

Or, god forbid, firing a shot in the air to warn me against wandering too far.

I can't help myself. It's just the two of us, and curiosity is killing me at this point. "Have you ever done this before? I mean, cooking food for somebody Lucian has staying here with him?"

"No, you're the first." If she thinks there's anything strange about that, I can't read it on her face as she plates my food. "Eat up. You could use a little meat on those bones."

It's not the first time she's said that to me, but I would rather not. It's not the weight that I need, anyway. It's nutrition, and I can't ignore how much better I've felt over this past week. I've slept better. I don't immediately crave caffeine in the morning just to get myself moving. It helps that I'm not working obnoxious hours, too. As a result, I've been able to rest, and as Lucian put it the last time we spoke, take care of myself.

And I can't even thank him for it. All I can do is wait for the rug to get pulled out from under my feet when he throws me out once he's tired of me. This is so fucked up.

I have more questions for Greta, but I doubt she would have the answers to them. What did I do to make him stay away from me? Did I insult him somehow? It didn't seem that way that last day. He was kind, gentle. He made me feel safe for the first time in... God, I don't even know how long. Maybe ever? At least since I was old enough to understand the way the world works and how much can be taken for granted.

A girl can get used to that sort of thing. She might even decide she likes the feeling and wants more of it. So what does he do? He takes it away. He takes himself away. I feel like I'm walking a tightrope all over again, only I don't know what's under me. Is there a net? Or maybe a pit full of alligators? All I know is I can't look down, or I'll fall.

I thank Greta for breakfast and leave the kitchen. It's almost easy to imagine parties here, with everybody laughing and toasting while gathered around the long, marble-topped island. Lucian doesn't strike me as the type of person to have big family events, though. I don't even know if he has a family. There certainly aren't any pictures of anybody anywhere in the house.

That makes me wonder. There has to be something around here to give me some clue about him, about the person he really is. From what I've seen so far, everything in the house could have been put together by an interior decorator, or maybe somebody who dresses sets for TV shows and movies.

There's no heart in it. No personal touches. If I had Lucian's money, you best believe I would take my time with a house like this. I would make it mine. I would fill it with me. I would also try to spend some time there when I could, but he doesn't do that, either. And maybe that's the problem. He's hardly ever here, so what does it matter if the house says anything about who he is? So long as it's clean, I guess.

Still, I have to search. I have to know. Otherwise, the questions are going to drive me crazy. I go from room to room, exploring, my footfalls echoing. The dining room, where it looks like thirty people could sit at the table all at once and still have plenty of elbow room. The library, where I've spent a couple of afternoons in a chair by the window. There isn't even anything special about the books—some of them, I noticed, look like they've never been opened.

All of this is fake, too. Set dressing. Like he wants to put an image of himself out into the world, even if he never lets the world inside.

Downstairs is an impressive wine cellar and a home gym that looks like something people would pay membership fees to visit. I'm sure he must spend time down here, being as fit as he is. I run my hands over a few of the machines, wondering when he used them last. The attached sauna must get some use, too. I'm sure he wouldn't mind if I tried it out, but I've never been in one before and don't know what to expect.

I'm not about to go to one of the guards and ask them for help; that much is for sure. I'm still unsure if they're even allowed to talk to me.

On and on I go, eventually moving up to the second floor, to the bedrooms. It's like moving through a museum, everything so quiet and so impeccable. Everything set up for guests he'll probably never have. I wonder if the housekeepers change the bedding even though it isn't used. Lucian strikes me as the type of person who would want that, just in case visitors might arrive.

He may not be great at knowing how to entertain a guest, but he does seem to believe in making them comfortable. I can't complain about that.

Finally, after what feels like hours—there's a ton of ground to cover—I reach the only set of rooms I've been told never to go into. Again, the whole *Beauty and the Beast* thing runs through the back of my head. He can't keep anything really horrible in there, can he?

No. He's not a monster. He's not a sweetheart, either, but I can't make him out to be a serial killer or something just because he wants his privacy. I'm sure there aren't bodies in there or torture devices. Though I don't think anybody could blame me for wondering. A girl could wonder a lot of things after living through this situation.

The hall is empty without a guard in sight. I hold my breath just to be sure there isn't a noise coming from someplace. Nobody on the stairs or lurking in the shadows. If I'm ever going in there, now's the time to do it. I won't take long. I only want to get a look at how he lives with the door closed and the rest of the world on the other side. What makes him tick?

I touch my hand to the doorknob.

"What are you doing?"

Son of a bitch.

I recoil from the door like it gave me a shock and spin on my heel. For one brief, heart-stopping moment, I expect to find Lucian at the top of the stairs. Glaring at me, fists clenched, jaw tight enough to crack walnuts. I can almost feel what he'll do to my body as punishment for this.

I wish I didn't almost like the idea.

It's only one of his many guards. I don't know their names, and frankly, I don't want to. I can't get Alexei out of my head, that damned liar. Whenever I start to break down and consider Lucian as being human, I remember what his guys do for him and snap out of it.

"I was…" I mean, it's obvious what I was doing, isn't it? "I hoped he might be home. I haven't seen him in so long, and I thought—"

"He ain't in there." He jerks his thumb in the opposite direction toward my room. "But he sent you something." I guess he was leaving it for me while I argued back and forth over whether I should explore Lucian's suite.

I know better than to take my time. Trotting down the hall with my head down. Good thing I never opened the door. I hope he doesn't report back to Lucian on this.

There's a long box on the bed with a smaller one beside it. I open it with trembling hands, holding my breath in anticipation.

Inside is a long black, one-shouldered dress. It shimmers when I hold it up to the light. I bet it'll move like water over me. In the smaller box is a pair of strappy stilettos. I guess this is my outfit for this evening? I can't help the little tingle of excitement that I won't be alone anymore.

There's a note tucked into the tissue paper. *Meet me at the club tonight for number three.*

14

Lucian

Tapping the pencil against my desk intently, I read over the new contracts. My mind keeps wandering to Rowan, and I skim over the words instead of letting them sink in.

"You seem distracted," Alexei says, calling me out.

"Because I am." There is no reason to lie to him. "The girl has been getting under my skin. I don't like it. She is on her way over here now. I just need to fuck her out of my system."

"If you say so." Alexei tips back his chair, balancing on the back legs like he is in fucking high school and annoyed by his math teacher.

"What's that supposed to mean?"

"I think there is more to it than sex. I've never seen you like this. The girl has gotten under your skin all right, but there is no way you are fucking her out of your system."

"I don't do girlfriends," I say more to myself than to my second in command. He knows how it is. We don't have time for that shit.

"You are doing something—"

"Join me tonight," I interrupt, making Alexei's eyebrows shoot up in surprise.

"You want me to fuck her with you?"

"Yes. Downstairs," I confirm.

"You don't have to prove anything to me. We don't have to do this," he tells me, but he can't hide the excitement in his voice. We have shared women before, and it was never disappointing.

"I know I don't have to do anything. I just want to. I only have two more times left with her. Might as well make it count."

Alexei nods his head, a smile tucking on his lips, and there is a knock on my office door. Rick comes in a moment later. "She is here."

"Let's go then," Alexei announces, clapping his hands together and getting up from his chair. He leaves the office eagerly as if he can't wait to get down there. Truth be told, neither can I.

We find her sitting at the bar, sipping on some fruity cocktail with a little umbrella hanging on the rim of the glass. She straightens her spine as soon as she sees us approaching.

"Finish your drink," I order a bit too harshly, making Rowan jump.

"Is everything okay?" she asks, her eyes bouncing between Alexei and me.

"Yes, Alexei is going to join us downstairs," I explain, watching Rowan's face go pale. I'm not sure what she is more scared of, going downstairs or having another man join us. "Have you ever had a threesome?"

To my surprise, Rowan nods her head yes, then lifts the glass with her now shaking hand and brings it to her painted lips. She downs the whole drink before asking me a question. "Does it have to be downstairs?"

"Yes." I nod. If I didn't enjoy her fear so much, I would tell her there is nothing to worry about. I won't physically hurt her. All I want is control. I don't get off by hurting women other than the kind of pain that gives them pleasure as well.

Placing my hand against her lower back, I gently push her off the barstool and lead her toward the stairs. She is hesitant, clearly scared of what's about to happen, and that fact has my dick pressing against my zipper painfully.

Alexei follows closely behind us as we descend to the basement level. By the time we reach the bottom of the staircase, Rowan's whole body is shaking. I nod to the door I want Alexei to open, and he does so quickly.

I lead Rowan inside, and she leans into me like she is worried she might pass out. Her eyes scan the area frantically, probably checking for some kind of torture device, but all that's inside this room is a single piece of furniture in the center. It's a custom-made sex bench that can be adjusting for multiple positions.

"Alexei, help Rowan out of her clothes," I order, drawing a little surprise gasp out of Rowan. "I told you he'll join us."

I let go of Rowan, and she basically stumbles into Alexei's arms. He catches her and starts pulling off her dress right away. I watch them curiously, wondering if Rowan will ask him to stop; then I remember she admitted to having had a threesome before, so maybe the only reason she is scared is being down here.

It doesn't take long for Rowan to be completely naked, her clothes in a small heap next to her feet. She steps out of her shoes, holding on to Alexei's shoulder for support, and for the first time tonight, a sliver of jealousy flickers through me. I don't mind sharing her sexually, but I don't like seeing any kind of affection between them.

"Get on the bench, ass up," I demand, making her flinch again. She hesitates, glancing between Alexei and me one more time before padding to the bench, getting onto it slowly. I let her take her time, not wanting to rush anything.

Once she is in position with her stomach on the bench and her knees propped against the bottom part, I crouch beside her and start fastening the leather cuffs around her ankles. Alexei goes to do the same on the other side without me having to ask.

"Do I have to be tied up? I won't move, I swear." She sounds desperate, but she doesn't move.

Instead of answering her, I keep tightening the restraints until they are snug enough so she can't pull out of them. She sighs and slumps against the bench in defeat. Straightening up, I run my hand along her naked backside, all the way from her plump ass to her shoulder blades. She shudders and lets out a little whimper.

I crouch down again, tying her wrist to the bottom of the bench while Alexei does the same on the other side. Her head is turned toward me, tears building in her eyes. Without words, she is pleading with me not to hurt her, but I can't tell her that.

"I'll give one choice today. Only one, so choose wisely," I say as I stand and walk toward the hidden wall closet. As soon as I open it and the large shelving with sex toys comes into view, I can hear Rowan struggle against her restraints.

"Please, don't do this," she starts begging.

"You don't even know what we're going to do yet." I pull out a vibrating butt plug, lube, and an open mouth gag. "Here is the choice you can make. You can either have this in your ass, and we take turns fucking your cunt, or I shove this in your cunt, and we fuck your ass?"

Her eyes go even wider as she considers my question.

"Tick tock, Rowan. I'm about to gag you, and it will be hard to understand anything you say once you have a cock in your throat."

Alexei is already taking off his pants, his dick hard and ready as I position himself in front of her face. Her eyes ping pong between the plug in my hand and Alexei's cock in front of her.

"Plug in my ass," she blurts out, her voice shaky.

"Ass it is." I nod, handing Alexei the gag.

I watch him put the gag ring into her mouth, so she is forced to keep it open. He fastens it around her head, making sure it's tight enough but not too tight. Rowan is breathing heavily, her body is shaking, and her eyes are pleading.

"Fuck her face," I order Alexei, who is all too eager to oblige.

Cradling her head in his large hands, he angles her face so it's lined up with his cock. She whimpers as he pushes into her mouth, her eyes finding mine one last time, begging me not to hurt her.

I remain still, watching as Alexei thrust into her throat until she gags. She closes her eyes, tears running down the side of her beautiful face.

"Fuck yeah," Alexei groans, shoving into her throat deeper and harder.

Slowly, I walk around until I'm behind her. Her ass bounces slightly every time Alexei thrusts into her. When she gags, I can see her puckered hole constrict as her whole body convulses.

Fuck, that's gonna feel great around my dick.

Flipping the cap of the bottle open, I pour a generous amount of lube over her ass and the plug. I take my time working it in her ass, enjoying the way her puckered hole opens up and gives way to the intrusion while the sound of her gagging on my friend's cock fills the room.

Once the plug is fully seated, I free my own cock and bring it to her waiting cunt. Lube from the plug drips down to her pussy, making me glide in with ease. In one hard thrust, I am all the way inside her. Rowan whimpers and struggles against the restraints, but I won't show her any mercy, not today... or ever.

"Fuck, your cunt is even tighter with this plug in your ass," I grunt.

Dropping the bottle of lube, I grab onto her hips and start fucking her furiously. My balls slap against her skin as I dig my fingers into her flesh with bruising force. Alexei and I fall into a rhythm, alternating thrusts.

Slowing down just a bit, I snake my hand around her front, find her clit, and start rubbing punishing circles over it. It doesn't take her long before her distraught whimpers turn into moans.

"Be a good fuck toy and come for us," I order, and she does almost immediately. Her whole body tightens, and her thighs quiver with her release.

Her cunt is squeezing me so tightly, I know if I don't slow down, I'm gonna come soon.

"Let's switch," I tell Alexei. He looks over at me, giving me a quick nod.

I pull out of her and walk around to her front while Alexei takes his place behind her. Rowan's head is hanging low, spit dripping from her open mouth as she catches her breath.

I take her head between both hands and force her to look at me. "You like getting fucked from both sides? Having all of your holes filled?"

She doesn't nod or shake her head. Instead, she simply looks at me through teary eyes. "You look so beautiful right now. Tied up with your mouth forced open—completely helpless." I wipe her tears with my thumbs and lean down to kiss her forehead. It's an oddly gentle gesture compared to the rest of what we're doing to her body.

When I stand back up, I guide my cock to her mouth and slowly press in. Her tongue caresses the underside of my cock, and my balls ache for release. I flex my hips and shove my cock into her wet mouth until I feel the back of her throat.

Heaven... that's what this feels like. Pure heaven.

Her throat is trying to push me out, but I keep forcing my cock down as far as she can handle. Every time I pull out, she gasps for air, coughing out spit.

"I think she is ready to come again." I let her catch her breath for a few moments and wipe her hair from her face. "Alexei, turn on the plug."

Her eyes blink open, finding mine immediately. There is an unspoken question in her gaze, but I don't have to answer because Alexei is already switching on the plug.

The low buzzing sound of the vibration fills the room, and Rowan moans in response. Alexei chuckles as he continues fucking her pussy.

"I'm gonna fuck your face until you come on my friend's cock. I'm not gonna stop for you to take a breath, so you better come quickly."

Rowan looks up at me through her wet lashes, fear flickering through her eyes as she shakes her head no.

I hold her head still between my hands and thrust into her mouth once more. Then I do exactly what I promised.

I start fucking her face without mercy.

15

Rowan

Lucian is relentlessly fucking my face while Alexei is using my pussy for his pleasure. The butt plug vibrates in my ass and is shoved deeper each time Alexei thrusts into me.

I can't breathe. Panic claws its way through me as I desperately try to suck in some air, but there is no room. Lucian has his cock so deep down my throat that my windpipe is constricted.

Struggling against my restraints, I say a silent prayer, hoping that he was joking. He has to let me breathe. He has to.

"Come, slut. Come for us," Lucian growls, his voice barely his own. He sounds primal as though he is barely holding on to his sanity.

My vision goes black, stars dance before my eyes from the lack of air. I'm certain I'm about to pass out. Then it happens. I come. I come so fucking hard I forget where I am. It's like an out-of-body experience. I'm floating in nothingness, wrapped up in pure ecstasy.

I'm vaguely aware of Lucian coming in my mouth; the salty taste of his cum lingers on my tongue as he pulls out.

My entire body goes slack, every muscle in my body is depleted, and I feel boneless. Alexei keeps rutting me from behind while Lucian frees me from the gag. My jaw aches as I try to close it, and Lucian massages my cheeks as I'm still trying to come down from whatever high I just experienced.

"I think she can come one more time, milk my cock dry as I fill you up," Alexei grunts behind me.

"No," I whimper, shaking my head. "I can't."

"I think you can." Lucian lets go of my head, and I let it fall onto the bench, my cheek pressed against the leather.

He moves to my side, and his fingers find my oversensitive clit, no matter how much I protest and try to squirm away. My whole body spasms with each touch, and all I want is for this to stop.

It's a nightmare, but I can't wake up. Having no control and nobody caring about what I want or need. I've had dreams like this before, but nothing as real, as painful, or as completely hopeless as this.

It's all too much, and I can't take it anymore. I'm sobbing, begging, feeling like my body is going to rip apart if they don't stop soon.

It doesn't matter. It's like I'm here, but I'm not. Like I don't matter. They could kill me, and it wouldn't matter so long as they get off.

The worst part is, I can feel another orgasm coming on, and I don't want it. It hurts; everything hurts. I'm too sensitive, so the slightest touch feels like an electric shock.

"Please!" I scream at the top of my lungs. "It hurts! Stop!" But then anything else I might've screamed gets pulled away when another orgasm shoots through me, making every muscle tighten, making me spasm uncontrollably. It's torture—that word keeps running through my head as my body shakes from the force of my release.

Somewhere in the background, I hear their laughter. They're proud of themselves for breaking me, for forcing me to come, for humiliating me.

But it still wasn't enough for them. They're not going to stop. They're never going to stop. All I can do is weep, too tired to fight back. Too tired to scream anymore. I'm broken. The little trust I had in Lucian is broken.

That must be what they were going for since they finally stop after the last orgasm. The room goes quiet. The tears that fall from my eyes now are those of relief because it's finally over. I'm so weak I can't even raise my head. I can't move a muscle. Then suddenly, gentle hands untie me and lift me off the bench.

I'm cradled against Lucian's chest as he murmurs sweet nothings in my ear. I don't want his kindness now. I don't want anything from him anymore. My lips part, and I want to tell him to leave me be, to go away, but my eyelids flutter closed, and I fall into the abyss of darkness before I get the chance.

The last thing I see is Lucian's stupidly handsome face looming above mine.

∼

WHERE ARE THEY? That's the first thought that goes through my head when I open my eyes, what has to be hours later. My body tenses in preparation for what's to come. As it turns out, there's no need for that because I'm back in my bed.

I shake my head. No, not mine. In Lucian's house. I have to stop thinking of it as mine—especially after last night. It feels like it happened to somebody else, not to me. No way could I have lived through something like that. The humiliation, the pain, the helplessness. The sense of being completely ignored and disregarded. I trusted Lucian, and I was stupid to do that.

I look down at my body, almost expecting to find it dirty and bruised. Instead, I'm dressed. I'm guessing Lucian cleaned me up and put my pajamas on me. He even tucked me in like he did back at my place. Like he got tired of playing with his toy and put it back for safekeeping. Did he kiss my forehead this time? I run the back of my hand over it, disgusted.

My eyes land upon a note on the nightstand: *Three down, one to go.* Bile threatens to race up into my throat, and I crumple the note in my fist.

Funny how the note I got with the dress and shoes excited me a little. It made my heart beat faster, made me bite my lip in anticipation. I can't pretend I haven't enjoyed our time together so far—at least, that was the case until last night. Last night was a totally different situation, and I don't think I can go through that again.

The only problem is, will he care? I don't even know if I have the guts to say it out loud. What will he do? How will he react? I've seen his temper. I've seen that look in his eyes that makes me think he's going to kill somebody.

I don't want him to look at me that way, God knows. But I also know I can't go through it again. My body, my soul, it's too much to handle.

And I'll hate myself if I don't at least speak up. I have to. I owe myself that much. Even if it pisses him off. I at least have to remind him that I'm a human being. I'm not just a few holes that can be filled whenever.

Screw the bath today. I'm not in the mood for a long, luxurious soak. Showering takes effort—even after sleeping for hours, hours in which I don't think I moved once—because I'm ridiculously sore all over. It takes longer than it should to wash and shampoo my hair. Even keeping my arms over my head takes effort. It's as though I've just been through a strenuous workout.

The items in the vanity don't strike me as nice or thoughtful anymore. They were always tinged with uncertainty, anyway, seeing as how they must've come my way after somebody broke into and went through my apartment. Now I can't bring myself to touch them. All of this is like some big, gorgeous wedding cake full of poison.

Once I'm dressed, I make it my mission to find one of the guards. They're so sneaky, all of them. None of them is exactly a small guy, either, which makes it even stranger to me that I rarely see or hear any of them. I only feel myself being watched.

I finally run into one of them outside, where it looks like he's waxing one of Lucian's many cars. "I need to see Lucian."

It's not so easy to stand up straight and tall with my chin raised when he looks at me. I might as well be a bug he wants to squash under his shoe. "What?" he grunts.

"I said, I need to see Lucian. I need to get in touch with him. Can you take me to him?"

He finally stops what he's doing long enough to look me up and down. One of his eyebrows arches. "You know what you're asking me?"

"Of course, I do. I need to talk to him. Can you take me to him?" I then look to the right and left at the other cars waiting to be waxed. "Or I could take one of these myself. I do know how to drive, even if my car isn't here."

"No, that's not gonna happen." He folds his massive arms over an equally massive chest. "I'll let him know you're looking for him."

"Thank you. Please, tell him it's very important. I have to see him right away." I can only hope he does what I ask, that he doesn't treat this like it's some kind of game. I can see how it would be easy to do that—to pat me on the head and send me on my way, knowing my word means nothing around here. Lucian is the one calling the shots. I might as well be a toddler who can scream and kick all she wants but who's never going to be treated as equal.

I spend an hour waiting in the library, flipping through the pages of a book without really reading any of it. I can't focus my thoughts on anything but whether or not he's going to come. And if he does, what will happen. I'm sure he doesn't like being interrupted.

What's the alternative, though? Waiting a week? Or maybe even longer this time. There's no guarantee when he's going to decide he wants me again.

And the thing is, I might not know he wants me until it's too late. He might spring out of nowhere and pin me down, and by then, it will be too late to tell him I don't want him to ever, ever do to me again what he did last night.

I'm actually starting to doze off a little when the door opens. I jump, startled, my heart in my throat, looking up in time to see Lucian striding into the room. I can't read his face. Is he pissed off? Concerned? Hell, for all he knows, he might've seriously injured me last night. That might be what I'm calling him here for.

He comes to a stop in the middle of the room, arms spread. "Well? Now that you interrupted me, why don't you tell me what's so incredibly important?"

The fact that he can stand there and talk to me that way tells me he still doesn't see me as a person. He can't, not after what he's put me through. And it doesn't matter that he tucked me into bed like last time. Eric was also nice to me after he beat the shit out of me. It's like I exchanged one of them for another just like him.

"I'm not doing this anymore."

I didn't even mean to say it that way, but now I'm pissed off, too. And something is satisfying about the way his face falls. I finally figured out a way to knock him off balance.

"Excuse me?" he finally sputters. "Not doing what, exactly? Living in my house? Having free run of the place? Or maybe it's the clothing you're wearing. Maybe that's what you don't want anymore."

"I never asked for any of this. I'll happily give it back to you right now if you want." I stand, unbuttoning my jeans.

"Stop it. You're being childish."

"No, I'm not. I'm standing up for myself. There's a difference." And now that I've gotten started, it feels damn good. I could get used to this. "And I mean what I say. I can't do this anymore. Last night was too much. I'm going back to my place."

He looks at me like he can't believe what I'm saying. "There was nothing in our agreement—"

"I understand that. But I don't think it's exactly fair. I had no idea what I signed up for, and you know it. How can I walk into a situation knowing my voice doesn't matter? You could end up killing me for all you know."

The bastard even has the nerve to scoff. "You were perfectly safe at all times."

"That's not how it felt. You have no idea how it felt. But what made it worse was being ignored. Like it didn't matter. Like I didn't matter." I put a hand on my chest, and it's only when my voice cracks a little that I realize how deeply he affected me. How hurt I am on a level much deeper than anything physical.

There I was, thinking I meant something to him, and then he turned around and did that. Completely disregarded me because he was having too much fun to stop.

"I want to leave. I want to go back to my apartment."

"Absolutely not."

"You didn't tell me I was going to be a prisoner when you brought me here!" I'm practically shouting now, but I don't care if anybody hears. Let them hear. Let them know how much I don't want this. "Thank you for what you've done for me, really. But for one, I didn't ask for any of it. And two, this can't go on forever. I have to get back to my own life, get a job and rebuild everything I've lost."

He doesn't say anything right away. I don't know if that's because he's trying to control his anger or because I've completely blindsided him. I doubt he's used to people standing up to him, telling him what they want. Denying him.

He'd better get used to it.

When he does speak, there's a dangerous note in his voice. It's too flat, too even. "May I remind you of our agreement? The terms of it?"

"The terms didn't include me staying here under lock and key."

He inclines his head. "You're right about that."

"So I should at least be able to go home. Have a little bit of control over my life, you know?"

"And what about the threat to your life? Has that suddenly ceased to be a concern?"

"I'll do what I have to. I'll move someplace else."

"I'm afraid that will be impossible. You still owe me an encounter, and if you skip town without making good on that, I'm afraid I'll have to send my men looking for you. Trust me. They're very good at finding people."

Him and his fucking encounters. "Fine. If that's what it comes to, you can have the money back. I haven't spent any of it. So long as my debt is cleared, we're even. I don't owe you anything."

No, I don't want to do that. But it's my last hope. If I don't owe him anything, he has no claim over me. I was hoping I wouldn't have to draw that card, but he's not exactly giving me any choice.

I can see the wheels turning in his head. What's he thinking? I'm almost afraid to find out. But at least I'm standing my ground. At least I can say that much.

He shakes his head. "I can't allow that."

My heart sinks. I can't say I'm surprised, but I was sort of hoping. "Why not? That would make us even, right?"

"This isn't a matter of being even, Rowan. It's a matter of fulfilling your obligation. You have an obligation to me, and you agreed to certain terms. What did I tell you the night we first met?"

"But you bent the rules, didn't you?" His brows knit together, and I know he knows what I mean. I jump on it, taking advantage. "You can bend the rules when you feel like it. Like you did when you told that guy to stop cutting me. Can't you bend the rules now? It went too far last night. I can't let myself go through that again. I've already spent too much of my life letting other people push me around and tell me what to do. I'm not going through that again." I lift my chin a little. "I would think after seeing for yourself what I've gone through, you would be able to respect that a little."

"Do not compare what I did to you to what your limp dick of an ex did. We made you come three times. We made you come so hard you passed out. I took care of you after. Washed and dressed you, tucked you into a bed, and covered you with a three thousand count thread Egyptian cotton sheet. You act like I beat you and threw you into some dungeon."

I huff, frustrated that he doesn't understand why I'm upset. "I know you didn't hurt me like he did, but you hurt me in a different way, and you treat me—"

"I think you fail to see something important," Lucian cuts in before I can finish. "The way I treat you when we have sex and the way I treat you at any other time is not the same. I have very specific tastes when it comes to sex, and you agreed to fulfill them. So all you have to do is keep those two separate."

I look at him dumbfounded. How in the world was I going to keep it separate?

"How about this." He slides his hands into his pockets, which I guess is better than tightening them into fists. "You stay and fulfill your end of our agreement, and we'll use a safe word this last time. That way, when you use it, I'll know it's time to stop."

It's tempting. I don't want to give up the money, so this might be a way around that. If I at least have a word I can use to bring everything to a stop, I'll have a little bit of power in the situation. That's better than nothing. "And you promise that if I use that word, you'll stop? No questions asked?"

"No questions asked."

"Okay. I can live with that."

He smiles, satisfied. "What would you like the word to be?"

I shrug. "I don't know. Red?"

"Fine. Red it is. You say that word, and the fun stops." He raises an eyebrow. "Anything else? Or can I go back to my day?"

He always has to have the last word, doesn't he? "No, that's it. Thank you for taking time out of your busy schedule." That might've come out a little sarcastic, and maybe I shouldn't have done it. But there's a bit of a smile at the corners of his mouth when he turns away, so I have to wonder if he minds all that much.

16

Lucian

There's a chill in the air tonight. It's clear, without a cloud in the sky, and the full moon casts its light over the woods. I chose tonight specifically because I knew the weather would be clear, that the moon would light the way.

She has to be able to see just enough to believe she can get away. And I have to be able to see enough so I can catch her, though I don't doubt I'll be able to do that without much trouble. I know these woods like the back of my hand, while I doubt she's ever been out here. She's in for quite a night.

And so am I. My last night with her.

As always, my mind rejects this idea. Nevertheless, I knew it was coming, knew that eventually, we would have to go our separate ways. There would eventually be a final encounter, one last time.

And I knew then, as I do now, that I cannot accept that. There's no way this is the end. There can't be an end, not at all. Because now that I've had her, I can't go the rest of my life without her. I could hire anyone to do what I make her do, could pay them any amount of money, but I would never find the satisfaction I find when I'm with her. There's something about her in particular that makes everything... More. Stronger, sharper, all-consuming. Better.

If she was willing to give the money back, that tells me it wouldn't be so easy to keep her. But I have to. There must be something I can do, something I can offer to make her want to continue this arrangement. More money? Certainly, her life could use an upgrade. I doubt she has much of an education, but I know she's been reading during her long, otherwise empty days. She's not a stupid girl. I could offer to fund her schooling, could subsidize her lifestyle so she wouldn't have to work. She could have a decent start in life, one which would've been impossible were it not for my generosity.

Surely, she can't be hoping to stay in that rathole of an apartment for the rest of her life. And eventually, once enough time passes, and she no longer hears from her recently departed ex, she'll come to understand he is no longer a threat. She will feel greater freedom. And then what? I could lose her forever.

I can't let that happen. What's that line from the movie? I'll make an offer she can't refuse. And if my first offer isn't good enough, then I'll make another, and another. Eventually, I will break her down the way I've broken her body for my pleasure. I will have what I want. What I'm starting to suspect I need.

Headlights in the distance catch my eye, and I watch as the two orbs of light grow larger. That has to be Rick—no one drives out here, especially in the middle of the night. There isn't a neighboring house or cabin for miles in any direction, which is how I like it. Even when I'm not using the house for activities like the ones I plan for this evening, I prefer to keep my distance from others. My idea of hell involves chatty neighbors.

Sure enough, a familiar SUV passes through a pool of moonlight, and I get a good look at it. My instructions were clear: drop her a half-mile northeast of the house. Then tell her to run. That's it. She'll be given no other direction but that. She has no idea where I am or even that I'll be hunting her.

Tonight, it will be me alone. I'm not going to share her, not like last time. As enjoyable as that was, sharing doesn't come naturally to me. Especially when I've stumbled upon something remarkable. Something like her.

Anticipation quickens my pulse, and adrenaline begins running through my veins. It's been a long time since I've performed a hunt at night, and this is the perfect sort of night for one. I'll keep her guessing, keep myself at a short distance long enough to give her hope that she might escape me. Of course, there is no hope. I hold all the cards.

In the back of my mind, I can't let go of the idea that this could be our last time. That no matter what I offer, she'll refuse. That little flash of independence she revealed in the library changed the game and left me wondering about her. It seems that no matter how much I learn, there's always more to know. Now I see she'll never be some trembling, weeping, thankful waif I rescued from a life of unspeakable pain.

I can't pretend I didn't know that spirit was somewhere in her. I admired it from our first encounter. Even though she was afraid of me that night in my office, she didn't cower. She didn't cry. She accepted the situation even though it terrified her. It was charming, then intriguing, almost delightful.

My attitude has changed.

The car pulls to a stop, not fifty yards from where I'm standing, half-hidden in shrubs. The woods are thinner here, which is why I wanted him to drop her in this place. It's deceptive enough to lead a person to believe the going will be easy with so many thin, scattered trees around. Twenty or thirty yards in any direction, however, tell a different story. The woods close in fast, and they're thick. Sometimes impenetrably so. Only the barest hint of moonlight will filter through the branches, and everything will look the same. She won't be able to tell where she's been or whether she's doubled back on her tracks.

I'll easily outmaneuver her in a pair of hiking boots I typically wear while staying out here. The only thing I'm carrying is a coil of rope. It's all I'll need.

I can hear her voice, can hear her asking questions as Rick pulls her from the car. The edge of fear in her voice is intoxicating. I can't deny it. She should be afraid.

Rick points away from the car. "Run!" He barks loud enough for the sound to carry my way on the evening air. She hesitates, but only for a moment, trotting off in the direction in which he pointed. I follow, careful to avoid making too much noise at first. I want this to unfold slowly, so I can't show my hand too early.

I can tell her heart's not in it. She's putting this on for show, pretending to run, looking over her shoulder with every other step. Almost like she's looking to see who's watching, to see whether she's giving a good performance. I deliberately step on a thick branch lying on the ground, and the satisfying cracking noise that results makes her jump. When she takes off again, she's moving faster.

I have the high ground, another benefit of knowing this land and all of its many features. She's coming up on a thin stream that cuts across the southern corner of the property. Her head swings back and forth as she decides which way to go. Should she follow the stream, or should she cross it? Already she's winded, doubling over with her hands on her knees to catch her breath.

I pick up the nearest rock and throw it into the stream not far from where she's standing. The splash makes her jump, and she takes off running again, following the path of the water. The ridge I'm standing on ends in another few hundred feet, so I have no choice but to make my way down the slope and follow her on lower ground.

She would never do well in an actual hunt; that much is for certain. She's sloppy, leaving a trail it takes no effort to follow. I can hear her up ahead, breathing heavy, like she's panicking. I laugh loudly enough for her to hear, and her sharp intake of breath tells me she didn't realize I was so close.

"You're going to have to be faster than that," I tell her, keeping my voice low. Menacing. The sound of feet crashing through brush grows louder, more desperate, and floundering. I follow with another laugh.

She crashes through the stream, then to the other side. I follow easily, jumping to the opposite bank with no trouble, now whistling softly as I trail her. "You can run, but you can't hide," I call out.

"Why are you doing this?" It's a breathless question, halfway between a demand and a sob.

"Trust me, Rowan. You don't want me to find you too quickly. You'd better run." She does as she's told, the way she always does, the way I can count on her to do. There's a fallen tree up ahead, and I watch as she hoists herself over it. I can only imagine her hands smart from the effort, along with the rest of her. That's nothing compared to what I have in mind tonight.

She stumbles and almost falls, and I deliberately pick up speed, letting her think I'm closing in. She scrambles to her feet and darts away, her golden head a beacon in the moonlight as she zigzags between the trees. She's becoming exhausted, I can tell, thanks to her panic and the physical exertion. Perhaps it would be better to take pity on her and bring this to a close.

Besides, I'm tired of waiting. Anticipation can only take a man so far before he becomes frustrated with it.

With that in mind, I take a long, curved arc, putting distance between us but knowing, in the end, I'm taking a shortcut. Another hundred yards in front of her is an old stone wall marking the southern edge of the property. Most of the wall has long since crumbled, but there's enough of it to provide a barrier against her moving forward. She can either go left or right. To the left is a mass of overgrown brambles I doubt she would take her chances with even if she wasn't half out of her mind with panic.

I wait for her by the wall, knowing she'll come straight to me. She doesn't disappoint and stumbles in my direction, not a minute after I reach the rocky surface. She can't see me, too busy looking around over her shoulder, deeper into the woods she only just stumbled out of.

So when I step out in front of her, she has no time to react. She slams into my chest and bounces off, landing on her ass. Before she can get away, I pounce on her, taking her by the arms and hauling her to her feet before locking my arms around her body, holding her fast.

"Gotcha." I can only laugh as she struggles in my arms, exhausting herself. The worst thing a person can do is try to use their head as a lever when someone has their arms trapped at their sides. It's completely pointless, and if a person struggles hard enough, they can knock themselves unconscious. Probably not the optimal result.

That's exactly what she's doing now. "That's right," I whisper in her ear. "Fight all you want. Maybe it will work this time. Maybe you'll be able to get away from me." She squirms harder than ever, but all she manages to do is rub against my cock, which was already semi-hard before I caught up to her. I should pull down her pants and fuck her here and now, in the dirt.

I'm not that crazy. And I don't much enjoy the idea of getting an infection—who knows what's out here in these woods? So I settle for wrestling her to the ground and pinning her with one knee on her lower back while she grasps and claws at the dirt.

I can't explain why this excites me the way it does, knowing I have her helpless and completely at my mercy. Knowing she's mine. For now, at least. She's mine and only mine, and nothing she will do can change that.

"Fuck you!" she barks when I reach down to brush her hair away from the side of her face. I only want to see her, to take in the sight of her flushed skin, her wide, fear-filled eyes scanning the area like she is expecting someone else to appear.

"It's just you and me," I croon. "You might want to consider speaking to me with respect, considering that there's no one here to help you, no one to save you. It would be much easier if you go along with it, Rowan."

She responds by kicking out when I touch her ankle. My grip tightens until she whimpers. "That's right," I mutter, binding her ankles together using the rope. "You're going to figure out who's in charge. It will go better for you if you treat me with a little respect. Maybe I won't fuck your ass until it bleeds."

She tries to scramble away with a high, shrill cry, but it's no use. I've already tied her ankles, and now I flip her onto her back. She punches, slaps, and claws at me, and I have to wonder in the back of my mind how much of this is sincere. Whether she's fighting for my sake or her own. Regardless of the reason, it's making me harder than ever.

"Every mark you leave on me will be one more mark I leave on you," I promise as I bind her wrists. She tries in vain to slip out of the rope as I stand, staring down at her. I could just as easily jerk off now, all over her, but that would ruin the fun. Why go to all the trouble of chasing her down while savoring the anticipation only to spike the ball short of the goal line?

The girl is as light as a feather, so it's easy to lift her and throw her over my shoulder. I find myself whistling happily as I begin the short walk up to the house. It's more of a cabin, really, though slightly better outfitted than one. I'm not a caveman, regardless of the fact I'm carrying a woman over my shoulder. I enjoy my comforts.

The anticipation builds the closer I get, and by the time I reach the shallow porch, I'm ready to blow a load in my pants. This is going to be a night worth remembering.

17

Rowan

Fear builds in my gut as the creaking of a door opening meets my ears. I'm breathing hard, my heart galloping in my chest. Yet I don't give up fighting—not to appease Lucian but because I'm truly afraid. Afraid of what he's going to do to me next.

I thought the basement in Purgatory was scary. I had no idea an even scarier place existed. At least at the club, there were other people, and I could hold on to the hope that someone would hear my screams.

Out here, there is nothing for miles. Nobody to hear me scream. For all I know, he could kill me and leave my dead body for the animals. No one would ever find me.

There's not too much I can see, even when Lucian flips the lights on. Just the wood floor and the corners of an armchair, a small table. A bed. Nicer than what I would expect out in the middle of nowhere. Great. I'll die in a nice bed.

He drops me onto it without warning, and I bounce hard enough to make me bite my tongue. It's uncomfortable, the way he's tied me up. He didn't play nice. My feet are starting to go numb. "Untie my legs, please. It's too tight."

His eyes are hard as he looks me over, walking slowly from one side of the bed to the other. "You think you deserve to tell me what to do? That's not how this works. You do what I want, how I want you to do it. And when I untie you, it'll be because I want to."

Right. We're still playing a game. I wish he would drop it. This is no fun for me, and I got all overheated and dirty out there. Not exactly sexy.

He seems to think so. When he turns to the side, his erection is obvious. His hand moves over it while I'm watching, and my eyes snap up to his face. "You don't want to watch me enjoy you?" He unzips, eyes moving over my body. "I have to do something about all those clothes. You're wearing too much. I need to see you."

I'm holding my breath when he kneels on the bed, waiting to see what he'll do. His hands are rough when he pulls my shirt up over my chest and then pulls down my bra cups until my tits are hanging out. My nipples go hard when the cool air hits them, and he takes one between his fingers and pinches until I whimper and arch my back, trying to roll away.

He takes his dick in his hand and starts stroking while playing with my tits. "I'm going to fuck that gorgeous mouth of yours, and you're going to take it." The next thing I know, he has a hand behind my head and guides his dick into my mouth. He sinks in before I can prepare myself, and I choke and gag.

It doesn't stop him. "Suck my cock," he whispers, hitting the back of my throat again and again. He buries himself so deep that my nose presses against him, and I'm afraid I'll suffocate. Just when I think I will and start to panic, he pulls out so I can breathe again.

It's such a relief when he pulls out. I have to gasp for air to keep from passing out. I barely notice him reaching over me to open a drawer next to the bed. Breathing is too good.

He's brutal when he pulls down my pants without untying my ankles. My thong follows them before he rolls me onto my stomach. "What are you doing?"

His answer comes when he grips my hips and pulls them back until my ass is sticking out. A buzzing sound fills the air. I try to twist my head around so I can see, but it's no use; he's out of sight.

"Let's get this pussy good and wet." He touches the vibrator to my clit, and I jerk in surprise, but he holds me in place with a hand on my lower back. "Relax and enjoy."

I don't have a choice. The deep, rumbly vibrations are strong enough that I'm already getting wet. I push back against the vibrator and moan as the tension ratchets up. He chuckles and turns up the intensity. I gasp loudly, but my pussy gets even wetter. I'm going to come soon if he doesn't let up.

It hits fast, hard, but there's no time to come down before the intensity ramps up again, and with it, the presence of something inside me. It's one of those rabbit things, with the clit tickler and dildo in one. Both of them are vibrating, and the dildo is rotating inside me, and it's too much already.

"What are you afraid of? Feeling good?" He moves the dildo in and out of me before pushing it in deep. Another orgasm starts again, building in waves that eventually crash into me.

"Stop, stop! I can't anymore!" All he does is laugh and leave the toy in place. His clothes hit the bed as he takes them off, and for a while, I don't know where he is. That's maybe the scariest part. Where is he? What's he planning next? I can't think about anything for long with my pussy convulsing the way it is, riding between pain and pleasure now that I'm so sensitive.

I could cry with relief when the toy slides out. "Let's get your ass ready for me." He smears my juices around my asshole—then slides the dildo into my pussy again before pulling my bottom half off the bed and setting my bare knees on the rough, wood floor.

He works his way in slowly, easing into my ass, but once he's in deep, he pulls back and goes in deeper. Hard. So hard it pushes me forward a little and makes my knees rub against the floor. There are splinters or something, and they hurt, but I can't move my legs. I can hardly move anything. Even my wrists are still bound, and they're pinned under my body.

It's sensory overload. I don't know if I'm feeling pain or pleasure the strongest, but all of it is mixing up, and I want it to stop.

Lucian doesn't notice any of it, fucking my ass until it hurts. But then the buzzing in my pussy pushes me closer to another orgasm while his thrusts shove me forward and into what I think might be a nail, not a splinter. A bent nail that's scratching my skin, pricking it, pressing into my knee.

"Such a tight little ass." Lucian smacks me hard with his palm, and I squeal. I might be coming again, but I'm starting to go numb down there. "My ass. Only mine." Another smack, even harder. I realize I'm crying. This has to stop.

Every time he thrusts into me, he pushes me harder and makes the nail dig deeper into my skin. I raise my head from the mattress and shout as loud as I can. "Please, stop! Stop, I'm hurt!" All I get for it is a slap on the ass that doesn't hurt as much as my leg does. "Lucian, stop!"

"Oh, no... you don't get to do that..." He wraps my hair around his fist and pulls my head back, leaning in to bite the side of my neck, then growls in my ear, "You're my slut. You do what I want."

"You're hurting me!" A sudden, sharper pain blasts through my leg, and I know the nail or whatever it is went into my knee. "Fuck, no! Stop!" I can barely hear myself over the squeak of the bed and the way he's grunting like a rutting pig every time our bodies crash together.

Then I remember. "Red! Red, red!" He has to stop now. He'll stop now. I brace myself and wait for it.

It doesn't come. He's not stopping. I can barely breathe, I'm crying so hard, and tears are soaking into the sheet under me. I suck in some air and scream, "Red!"

"So close." He yanks my hair again and breathes in my ear. "You're going to make me come, Rowan." I barely register this over the screaming in my head and the sickening beat of my heart.

He didn't stop. He's not stopping. I trusted him, but he's not stopping.

What else is this man capable of?

18

Lucian

SHE'S PERFECTION. Nothing less than that. The fulfillment of my every fantasy come to life. Like she was made just for me.

I come with a roar, filling her cunt until my cum drips from her when I withdraw my cock. There's a sense of satisfaction in that, in watching my seed drip from her. Because I've claimed her pussy. I've claimed her ass. She's mine.

With a sigh of satisfaction, I collapse at her side. I'm spent, truly and completely, a blank slate. As if every ounce of tension, concern, anxiety over every mundane, everyday bullshit has fallen away. There are no accounts to balance, no clientele to satisfy, no palms to grease. Just peace and quiet and stillness; it's euphoric, and it's all thanks to Rowan.

It takes a minute for me to come back to my senses, for my breathing to slow down, my thoughts to clear. I'm exhausted down to my bones. The evening's activities have left me spent—but happily spent.

It doesn't take long for me to realize I'm the only one who's happy at the moment. Once the pounding of my heart settles, and I can hear more than the rush of blood in my ears, the sound of broken sobbing makes its way into my consciousness.

I lift my head, rolling to the side toward Rowan. She's worked her way onto the bed, facing away from me, still bound as I left her. And sobs wrack her body, a gust of emotion that shakes the entire bed. How can something so small be so powerful? For a moment, I'm afraid she's having a seizure—but when I reach for her, my fingers barely grazing her skin, she jerks away like my touch is fire. So she is conscious, at least.

"Rowan. Look at me." All she does is shake her head, and her sobbing gets louder. This isn't put on. This isn't a show. This is the sound of a woman weeping for all she's worth, weeping like her heart has been broken.

For a moment, I consider letting her cry herself out, letting her get it out of her system before questioning her again. To try to talk to her right now would be a waste of time, anyway—she's in no condition.

I can't just leave her that way, though. Knowing there's something wrong. "Did I hurt you?"

All that question does is cause her to curl into a ball, bringing her knees up to her chest. I'm starting to become irritated, and she doesn't want that. "Can you talk to me?" Finally, after receiving nothing in response but fresh tears, I've had enough.

Despite her trying to flinch away, I turn her onto her back, so I can at least get a look at her face. When she tries to turn her face away, I take her by the jaw and tug.

She opens her eyes, and they find mine, and what I see there stirs something deep inside me. Something I didn't know existed, something that's never bothered me until now.

She's broken. I've never seen someone so broken. And I'm the cause of it.

"Please." It's barely a whisper, nearly inaudible. "Please, untie me. I'm hurt."

I do just that, confused by all this. Why do I care so much? So she had a rough time. Plenty of girls do. They're my stock and trade. What makes me more money than any of the vanilla kink my club provides. I've even participated with a few of my clients, and I've witnessed the depth of their depravity. I'm well aware of the depths of my own, too—that's one thing I've never kidded myself about. I know who I am, what I like, and what I'm willing to do to turn my fantasies into reality.

Why, then, do her tears stir up something like sympathy? I can't remember the last time I felt genuinely sorry for someone. She might be the first in years.

Once her hands are free, she examines her right knee. Now I see it's scratched and bleeding with what looks like a puncture mark. "There was a nail sticking out of the floor, and I tried to make you stop, but you didn't. How could you do that to me?" she whispers, rocking back and forth as if to comfort herself.

"What did I do? I thought—"

"You know exactly what you did. What was all that talk before, in the library?"

"I don't understand."

"The safe word!" she screams, her face going red. "It was your idea to have a safe word. All the shit you put me through tonight was okay because I told myself there was a safe word I could use. I could stop it if I needed to. But what happened when I used it? Nothing! You ignored me!"

She has me at a loss. I hardly remember the specifics of what just happened. Was I in a trance? Certainly, there've been times when I was at the height of arousal, and nothing else around me mattered much. When I was able to ignore everything else in the world but the sensations rolling through my body. When the only thing in the world was satisfaction, and I was just on the cusp of achieving it.

But I never completely lost myself. There's always been some sliver of my consciousness still alert, prepared to step in and take control if need be.

Did you ever intend on honoring a safe word at all? My inner consciousness recoils from the question, but there's no escaping it. Not with Rowan's hard, tear-filled, accusatory eyes boring holes into my skull. Is it possible I accepted her safe word as a way of shutting her up at the moment? A desperate attempt to keep her with me a little longer? Because I don't even remember hearing her say it, though I have no doubt she did. I lost myself. I had no intention of keeping myself under control tonight, and I realize that now.

And look what I did.

I'm not sure what to do now. It's rare for me to be in a situation like this, where there's any sort of need to apologize for wrongdoing. I don't apologize because I never think much about how my actions affect others. I live in a transactional world. So long as the books are balanced by the end of the day, I have no troubles.

This isn't so easy to balance. Judging by the way she glares at me while protecting herself from me, I wonder if there's any way I can undo what's been done.

I reach for her since that's what instinct tells me to do. I only want to hold her, to comfort her, to try in some way to explain what came over me tonight. There must be some way I can make her understand.

When she scrambles away from me, eyes filled with terror, I know it's no use. There's no coming back from this, at least not right now.

"Don't touch me." It's a hiss filled with all the venom of a snake prepared to strike. "Don't ever put your hands on me again. I don't know what I was thinking, trusting you. Why I wanted to believe you. I forgot who you are."

"And who would that be?" I ask, fighting to maintain my self-control.

"You're a monster. You get off on hurting people. You're no better than —" She cuts herself off, eyes darting away from mine. She's too smart to say it, though there's no question who she's thinking about. I wonder what she would do if I told her right now at this very minute what became of him. How much joy I got out of watching him get taken apart piece by piece in that little room. How the memory had fueled more than one jerk-off session in the days since then. Remembering his screams, his pleas, rolling them around in my head the way I roll an exquisite wine over my tongue.

She thinks I'm a monster? She has no idea.

Her jaw is set in a firm line. "That's it. That was your fourth time. This is over now."

How can she say that so casually? Like it doesn't matter?

"Well?" she demands. "Wasn't that the terms of our agreement? You're the one who's always bringing them up and throwing them in my face. How does it feel?"

"Rowan, I—"

"I don't want to hear it. I'm tired of listening to men tell me after the fact why they couldn't help but hurt me." She slides off the bed, hunched over in a defensive position, pulling herself together. She walks like someone in pain, and another sharp blade of guilt slices its way into my heart. I did that to her. She isn't some faceless, nameless stranger whose existence I was unaware of until this moment and will never cross my consciousness again.

"I'm going to my apartment. I'm not coming back to your house."

That causes me to wince. I'm glad her back is to me so she can't see. "Very well." What am I supposed to do? Argue with her? Beg her to return? I see now that trying to come up with an offer that would make her continue our arrangement was pointless. She was in it for money, nothing else.

And now, I get the feeling I've destroyed whatever might've existed between us. Any hope she might have reconsidered and agreed to continue our strange relationship is obliterated.

I get up, dressing quickly. I can't stand to be in this room, in this house, with her. There's too much guilt and shame in the air. It makes it difficult for a man to breathe. Yet I can't keep myself from sneaking looks at her, watching her as she slowly, carefully puts herself together.

"Is there anything else you would like to say to me? Anything you need to get off your chest?" This isn't a kind question. It's not made out of concern for her. So what is it, then? Maybe I want to punish myself. Maybe I deserve it. I must, or else why would I feel remorse?

Until this point in my life, remorse has been as remote as the moon now shining through the windows.

She turns her head slightly, just enough to catch me out of the corner of her eye. "I never want to see you again. Don't contact me. I want to forget this ever happened."

I take this as well as I can, nodding once before going to the door. "Rick will be back to take you home. Anything you brought to the house will be dropped off to you in the morning and left at your front door." She only grunts softly in response, which I choose to take as an affirmative before leaving her alone.

My car is parked behind the house, and I waste no time getting out to it. I text Rick that she is ready for pickup before I start my own car.

How could everything have gone so wrong? I can't shake the feeling as I drive home, passing Rick along the way as he goes to fetch her, that I've destroyed the best thing that's ever come into my life.

What a shame we only come to these realizations after the destruction has been done.

19

Rowan

How do I know if I have tetanus? That was the first thing on my mind when I woke up this morning—whether I might end up with tetanus because of that nail last night. Wouldn't that be hilarious in a completely fucked-up way? After all this, everything Eric and Lucian, and everybody else in my life has put me through, I could end up dying from some stupid, rusty nail.

I scroll through the links my question pulled up, then skim the first article. A person can get a tetanus shot within three days of a wound and still be okay. So at least I have that going for me. I'm not going to drop dead from lockjaw or whatever.

Though if I'm not worried about that, I have nothing else to do but think about other things. Remember them. Obsess over them.

How could he do that to me? And how could he act surprised when I called him on it?

I have to stop torturing myself about him. We're through. Finished. Four encounters and that's it. I should be dancing around the apartment right now. Maybe I would if I didn't have a fricking nail wound in my leg.

Maybe I would if the thought of never seeing Lucian again didn't make me feel sort of empty inside. Or like I'm dangling in midair. Waiting to drop so my feet will touch something solid again. It's not so much that I want to see him, really—I mean, he's the last person I want to see right now. But the sense of there being unfinished stuff between us makes me uncomfortable.

So does the wound on my leg. I should get it checked out and probably get a shot before my lungs stop working or whatever is supposed to happen. I didn't want to delve too deep into what the internet had to say because sometimes they like to sneak gross medical pictures in articles, and I hate those.

One problem: I don't have insurance. Not like a single shot should cost all that much, but who knows? And it's not like anybody will give me a straight answer if I ask before they stick me. Dammit, this isn't my fault. I didn't do anything to hurt myself. I tried to stop before the damn nail stuck me.

Lucian should pay for it. He has that doctor of his. She seemed legit enough. I wonder if she could help. Either way, this should be up to him since he's the one who hurt me.

I only have Alexei's number in my phone, though. So he'll have to put us in touch—no, better yet, he can pass the message on to Lucian. I don't want to hear his voice. It's not like I want to hear Alexei's, either, but either I deal with him or possibly get sick. I might have ten grand in the bank, but that doesn't mean I want to blow all of it on medical bills. "Alexei, it's Rowan. Can you do me a favor?"

He grunts. "Why would I do that?"

"Because I need a favor, and you're the only way for me to get in touch with your boss. I have to go to the doctor to get a tetanus shot after getting stuck with a nail at the cabin last night, and I'm not paying for it." Sure, that sounds strong and decisive.

He's quiet for a few seconds, and I'm afraid I crossed a line I didn't know existed. "Fine." And that's it. Call over. What am I supposed to do with that? It's not my fault Lucian didn't want me to have his number. It's okay for him to shove a plug up my ass, but god forbid I call him on the phone.

Maybe ten seconds pass before my phone rings. "Rowan. What is this about needing a doctor?"

The sound of Lucian's voice makes my heart race, and not in a good way. I feel a little sick, overwhelmed, jittery. "Like I told Alexei, I need a tetanus shot after getting hurt. I have no idea the last time I had one. Probably when I was little." All that fake strength I had with Alexei is gone. What is it about this man?

"Of course. You need attention. I should've thought about it last night." He sounds snappy, almost angry. At himself or at me? "I'll have Rick drive me over—"

"No. I don't want to see you. I'm not kidding. But I think you should have to pay for it."

"Right. It's only fair." It doesn't sound like he thinks it's all that fair. "I'll send Alexei." Why do I feel like he's punishing me? He's got to know I wouldn't want to hang out with Alexei, either. I doubt he will take no for an answer, though, so I don't bother fighting. What matters is getting to the doctor.

I end the call before he can pull me into a conversation I don't feel like having. What if he shows up anyway, even when I told him not to? What will I do? I'll have to figure it out, I guess. I don't owe him anything. He's not in control. I should be able to tell him to go fuck himself if he can't take no for an answer.

How much more could he do to me? Maybe I shouldn't think too much about that.

I'm watching from the window as a familiar black car rolls up to the curb in front of the building. Is he in there? I can't believe I'm holding my breath, but I am. I don't even know for sure whether I want Lucian to be in the car or not. No, I don't want to see him. But... I sort of do. I know that now. I can talk about closure all I want, but the bottom line is, I don't like the thought of never being with him again.

It's Alexei who steps out of the car and opens the back door. Nobody comes out. He's waiting for me. The text he sends a second later confirms it. *I'm here. Let's go.* Pleasant, as always.

I take my time, though. Just because he snaps his fingers doesn't mean I have to come running. I brush my hair, put on a little lip gloss, then slide into a pair of flats before grabbing my purse and heading for the door. Alexei scowls at me when I reach him. "Took you long enough." He waits until I'm in the back seat before slamming the door.

The energy in the car is sour, heavy. I stare out the window as he drives us wherever we're going. Why bother asking? It's not like I'll get a straight answer anyway. By the time we reach a small, brick office building in the middle of nowhere, we've been on the road for almost forty-five minutes. This isn't like the cabin situation, though. We're not in the woods. More like a secluded little hideaway with trees and a freshly mowed lawn the size of a football field.

I hesitate rather than getting out of the car right away. Alexei peers at me. "Well? You gonna get out or what?"

"Where are we?" There aren't any signs around saying this is a doctor's office or any kind of office. He could've brought me to some kind of torture chamber for all I know.

He nods toward the building. "It's where the doc lives. Boss set it up. She doesn't, you know, have an office." He clears his throat, and that sound expresses a whole lot of things he either doesn't want to say or isn't at liberty to explain. Either way, I get the message. A regular doctor doesn't make the sort of house call she did.

Here goes nothing.

∼

He's waiting for me outside the car, munching on an apple. There's something so normal about it, I could almost laugh. Sliding his aviators down the bridge of his nose, he looks me over. "You okay?"

"Yeah, she gave me a shot, made sure the puncture was clean. A little ointment for the pain."

"Good." He tosses the apple core into some bushes before moving toward the rear driver's side door—then stops when I hold up a hand.

"Can I sit up front with you?"

"Huh?"

"I hate riding in the back like that. It makes me feel weird." I can tell this is unusual for him. "Sorry. Didn't mean to short circuit your brain or anything."

All he does is sigh, closing the door before walking around the car and opening the passenger door for me. I climb in, and he closes it, then walks around again, muttering to himself. Probably wondering what he's supposed to do with me sitting next to him for the better part of an hour.

We're barely off the property before he asks if I'm hungry. I didn't expect that question. "Want to go to a drive-thru on the way back?" he suggests as we pull out onto the tree-lined road.

"Yeah, that would be good." I was a little too distracted to eat this morning. "Thanks."

"Sure." He taps his fingers against the wheel before reaching for the radio controls. "You want music?"

"If you want." He turns it on and finds something surprisingly quiet, sort of nice. Easy listening, I think they call it. It fits with the pretty area we're in. I can almost imagine we're on a nice country drive. "I wonder if people take them anymore."

"Hmm?"

I didn't mean to say that part out loud. "Drives. Just driving for the sake of driving. When I was little, we were pretty poor, and sometimes all my mom could afford to do was take me for a drive someplace. When gas wasn't too expensive."

"Too much other stuff to do." He snorts. "You can go on YouTube and watch a video somebody took of a drive they went on."

I can't help but laugh. "Right? It's so bizarre, like videos of people opening boxes. They're so popular. I don't get it."

"If there's one thing I've learned working for the boss, it's that you can't figure out what people are into."

"I guess you see a lot."

"I do." I can see him glancing my way from behind his sunglasses. "It's not always fun. I guess I want you to know that. We've all got shit we're trying to take care of, you know? Lucian pays well. That kind of money takes care of a lot of shit."

There's something in his voice I've never heard before. Like there might be a human being in there. "I never thought of it that way, I have to admit."

"Everybody's got a cross to bear. Something my mom used to say when I was a kid. She can't say much of anything anymore."

I think I get the message he's trying to send. He has people he takes care of. He was probably in the same sort of spot I was in or something close to it. Desperate. Who's going to say no to that kind of money when they have a shit ton of medical bills piling up? I know how that goes, for sure.

He looks my way again. "Shit went bad last time you were with him."

"Shit went bad the last two times," I point out.

"You mean when you passed out from an orgasm? Yes, it looked like you had a terrible time."

My face suddenly feels like it's on fire. Sometimes I forget that Alexei fucked me at the club. Probably my mind suppressing it.

"It was intense, you were overwhelmed, but you weren't hurt."

"No, not that time… but it's not just about physical injury; it's not just the nail thing. I trusted him, and he broke that trust—both times."

"So that's what made it so different for both of you?"

I nod slowly. "Is he pissed?"

"No. I wouldn't use that word—though if he is, I think he's more pissed at himself than anybody else. Not at you. He freaked out when I told him you wanted to go to the doctor. He went all pale."

It's tempting to imagine that. "Yeah, probably because he was afraid I'd sue or something."

"No. It wasn't like that. I've never seen him like this before."

I chew my lip as the scenery around us changes. There's a strip mall up ahead with a handful of chain restaurants in the parking lot. "Can we stop up there for a burger?"

He nods and pulls the car into the lot. It's no surprise that he orders two double burgers and an extra-large fry. I settle on a single burger and a soda.

It's strangely normal, sitting here like this. Eating fast food in a parking lot like we're just two people hanging out. Somehow, that gives me the courage to talk to him like I'd talk to a normal person. "What do you mean, you've never seen Lucian like this before? What's so different about him now?"

He snorts before polishing off his first burger. "He's different. I don't know. Like he really cares about you."

I can't believe how much I want to believe that. "He has an odd way of showing it, doesn't he?"

"He does, though. Just remember there might be things you don't know about."

Oh, that makes me feel a lot better. "Like what?"

"Just things." I'm pretty sure he finishes his second burger in all of three bites. "He cares a lot more about you than I've ever seen him care about anybody, and I've been working for him a long time. And no, he didn't tell me to say that, so don't bother asking."

That makes me laugh again because I was going to say something like that. "Fine. I'll trust you." Even if I don't know what to think about it. One more layer to the mystery that is Lucian.

By the time we reach my building, it's almost like we're friends. Every day brings a new surprise, I guess. "Thanks for the ride and for everything else." I even feel a little regretful, like I don't want to go back upstairs by myself. Since when is Alexei good company?

Something else hits me around the same time. I glance up at the window, wondering. "Would you mind coming up with me and looking around, just in case?"

"In case of what?"

"You know." Is he going to make me say it? "In case anybody is waiting for me."

"Like Eric, you mean?" He shakes his head. "Listen. I'm only gonna say it once. You don't have to worry about him ever again."

I take a step back, looking him up and down. "What's that mean?"

"It means what it means. You're safe now." He whistles softly to himself as he gets back in the car. "Go up. He'll be pissed if I don't tell him I watched you go in." He's probably right. I go in and hope he's right about me being safe, too.

When I open the door, I find a piece of paper on the floor, like somebody slid it underneath. That's not the only thing that catches my attention, either. The keypad mounted to the wall is new.

So is the furniture in the living room. Entirely new, down to the TV and the console it's sitting on. It's enough of a surprise to freeze me in place—though once the surprise wears off, I bolt for the bedroom. Sure enough, I have a new bed, a new dresser, and a nightstand. Everything's new, and it doesn't look cheap.

I finally think to take a look at the paper. It's from the security company that installed the alarm system I didn't order, explaining how to use it, how to set my code, all of it.

It wasn't enough to make sure I got to the doctor. He had to buy me an apartment full of new furniture and a security system, too. Is this what Alexei means when he says Lucian cares about me?

20

Lucian

"How is she?" I can't believe how it seems everything in my life hinges upon Alexei's answer. The way I've sat here, my guts churning, berating myself for hurting her. For being the reason she had to see the doctor. That's the last thing I want for her.

"Fine. Probably wondering where all that furniture came from."

I wave a hand at this. "She needed it. And the security system. God knows. But she's all right?"

"She's all right." I pretend not to notice the knowing little smirk he's wearing as he leaves my office. It eats me up inside, knowing how obvious it must be to everyone around me that Rowan is more than a financial transaction.

She's the only woman in my employment who's ever stirred more than my cock, and I let her down. I hurt her. She has every reason to hate me. Here I am, priding myself on discipline and control, and I hurt the only woman I've ever cared anything about.

Who am I? What does any of this say about me? I'm not who I thought I was. Above messiness, above feelings. Above guilt.

There's work to be done. Books to be checked, numbers to be run. It's days like this I wish I could hire someone to keep things going smoothly, but I don't trust anyone as much as I trust myself. This is too important to let some idiot screw up which set of books is which.

Though at the rate I'm going, I could very well end up being that idiot. I can't get Rowan out of my head. I'm staring at numbers, but all I see is her.

The hatred in her eyes. Cold, hard. The pain, thanks to me.

There I was, wondering if there was a way I could prolong our relationship. I know this is about more than fulfilling some kinky fantasy—there are countless women I could use for that, women who work under this roof. Women who will owe me money one day and just don't know it yet. There are countless ways to procure partners.

I don't want them. I want her. All of her, all the time. Every day. There has to be a way.

How does a man convince a woman to be in a relationship? The whole romance thing has never held much interest for me. I'm nobody's idea of a hero.

I already sent her an entire apartment worth of furniture. Not as a bribe but as a way to show I care. She hasn't even called to say thank you. I doubt she'd be any better impressed if I sent flowers, a car, the deed to a house. Besides, I don't want to earn her that way. She's worth more than anything money could buy.

Besides, something tells me she would see straight through it.

How does a man show a woman he wants nobody but her? I'm so desperate, even the idea of googling pops up in my head as an option.

The woman has no idea what she's done to me, how low she's taken me. Maybe we'll laugh about this one day.

"Boss? We've got a problem downstairs."

I press the button to open the door, rubbing my temples as I do. Like I need another problem today. "What is it?"

Alexei looks ready to kill. "Glen's back. He wants Rowan."

"Excuse me?" I stand slowly. "He wants what?"

"Rowan. He won't take no for an answer." He gestures toward the open door. "He's losing his shit down there. Screaming that he wants her, and he won't leave until he gets what he paid for."

I'll fucking kill him.

My arm sweeps over the desk, scattering everything across the floor. It doesn't do anything to calm the rage burning through me, white-hot flames scorching me from the inside out. To think he believes he deserves to touch her. To breathe the same air. She's so far above him; it's amazing he can even see her.

"I want him taken care of." I'm staring down at my desk and the wreckage all over the floor. "Now. Get him out of here and see to it he doesn't come back. He's not welcome here anymore." I lift my head, my eyes meeting his, so he knows I'm serious. "And if anybody else even thinks about touching her, I'll kill them—all of them. I want you to make sure everybody understands that from here on out. Got it?"

"Got it." There's even what sounds like satisfaction in his voice. The door clicks shut, and I'm alone with my rage.

There's only one way to quiet it. Not calling one of the girls up to dance for me. Not fucking someone, anyone, no matter how nasty I decide to get.

I decide to drive myself rather than asking one of the men to do it. They'll be busy with Glen. One less problem for me to think about. It isn't like we're hurting for the money he gladly hands over. And it's not as if there aren't ten freaks right behind him, glad to hand over any amount of money so long as they can get what they need.

It's late, at least for people whose work is done in the daytime. For me, eleven o'clock might as well be morning. It's the time things begin to get interesting around the club. Yet most so-called normal people are inside, watching the news or something just as boring at this time of night. Traffic is light as a result, and it takes no more than a few minutes for me to reach Rowan's building.

There's a light burning in her window. She's still awake. I don't know what to do now—for once, I didn't have the next step planned in advance. I want to go up there, but something tells me that would only make things worse. I don't need her using that expensive new alarm system to bring the cops over.

As it turns out, she makes up my mind for me. I've just decided to watch her window, to soothe myself with the knowledge that Rowan is safe and maybe jerk off in the car to relieve my tension when the front door to the building swings open and she steps out. She doesn't notice me, making a right turn at the bottom of the steps and heading down the sidewalk at a quick clip.

I can't stop myself from getting out of the car and calling out to her over the hood. "Rowan."

She stops dead, eyes going round when she spots me coming her way. "Stop. Leave me alone."

I finish rounding the car but stay back before she can scream and alert a passing driver. "What are you doing, going out at this time of night?"

She blinks rapidly, frowning. "I wanted a pint of ice cream and milk for tomorrow morning. What's it to you?"

Her flash of anger is a turn-on, honestly. I'd normally warn a woman against talking to me that way but coming from her, it's refreshing. I don't even blame her for it. Hell, I'm surprised she even says a word to me. This is better than nothing.

She's waiting for a response. "It's not safe for you to walk around at this time of night."

"I'm going to the corner." She folds her arms. "By the way, thanks for breaking into my apartment and having that furniture delivered. And the alarm system, very generous. I didn't ask for any of that."

"You didn't have to. It's what you deserve."

"What about last night? Is that what I deserved?"

"I can make it up to you."

She snickers. "Come on. Do you know who that sounds like? I've heard it before. I'll never do it again. I'll make it up to you." She holds up her hands, backing away. "No offense, but I'm not trying to get myself into the same fucked-up nightmare all over again."

"It wouldn't be like that."

"That's so easy to say."

"It's the truth. I'm not that kind of man. You should know that by now."

"I don't know any such thing. You lied to me. You told me what I wanted to hear so you could have what you wanted." Now she wraps her arms around herself, and I realize she's shaking. "You haven't proved you're a good man. I don't want to stick around and find out what else you're capable of."

"I'll prove it, then. We can come up with a new arrangement, and you can have a say in it." I have to hold back before I start babbling like some frantic idiot. She has far too much power over me, but there's nothing I can do about it. I'm too far gone.

For a moment, I think she might come around. It looks like she wants to. Like she's fighting with herself because, at her core, she knows I'm telling the truth. Because she wants it to be the truth.

"Rowan. You can trust me." I reach for her—sure she'll let me touch her—but she flinches away, shaking her head.

"No. I don't trust you." She backs away, farther down the sidewalk. "I need time. Leave me alone, please. I have to think things over."

"Just tell me there's a chance. That's all I need now, to know there's a chance of us working something out."

She bites down on her lip, brows drawing together. "I don't know. That's the best I can say. I don't know if there's any future here." With one more look, she turns away, walking fast with her head down. For once, there's nothing I can do but watch. For once, I can't make another person do what I want.

21

Rowan

My life is so incredibly fucked up. I should stop trying to make sense of it.

I spent one week virtually locked away in Lucian's mansion, and now I've spent the past week locked in my apartment.

All things considered, I'm not sure which place I like better. Sure, his house is ridiculously comfortable and much larger than any one single person needs. I had everything I could ever want or need at the tip of my fingers except for human interaction—though it's not like I'm getting any of that here, either, with my door locked against the rest of the world.

The bottom line is, I'm afraid. More afraid than I've been in a while—hell, even more afraid than I was of Eric sometimes. Eric never used me the way Lucian did. He might've hit me, and there were a lot of times I wasn't in the mood, but he convinced me to go along with it.

He wouldn't have continued fucking me as I screamed and wailed and begged. He would've stopped if I used a safe word. No, I have no way of knowing for sure, but I feel it.

Now I'm afraid to leave my apartment in case I run into one or the other. Eric hasn't shown his face since that day at the mall, and sure, Alexei told me I don't have to worry about him, but that's easy for him to say. He doesn't know Eric like I do.

And even I don't know what's going through his sick brain. He could show up any time. Or he might grab me out in the open like he did last time. I can't predict what he'll pull.

As for Lucian, I don't think he would ever stoop so low as to visit someplace I'd visit. Like he would ever go to the mall or out to a diner for something to eat. I'm sure he's too important to ever sit with other people in a movie theater. So I'm not worried about crossing paths with him out on the street.

But Alexei or one of the other guys? That's another story. For all I know, he'd have one of them follow me around because he's a sick fuck like that.

I have to ask myself why it matters if he wants to follow me or whether Eric still has a grudge he wants to work out on my face. They're both out of my life now, and I have ten thousand dollars sitting in the bank. If I have to, I'll find an apartment on the other side of the country and start a whole new life. We'll see how good Lucian's men are at finding people. Who the hell does he think he is, anyway?

I should've known better. I shouldn't have let myself forget who he is at his core. He doesn't care about people. He cares about his business and about himself, and that's all. Everything he showed me, everything he did—tucking me in, making sure I had clothes and makeup, even letting me stay with him so I could get away from Eric—all of it was for his benefit. Dressing me the way he wanted to dress me, keeping me waiting until he was good and ready to do some fucked-up thing to me.

For all I know, letting me stay at his house was just another way of controlling me. It might not have had anything to do with Eric at all. If anything, that might've been a nice excuse for Lucian to sweep in and pretend to be a hero.

And to think, he actually acted like he had no idea why I was upset. He must not have listened to me at all when I told him I wasn't going through that again. There I was, so proud of myself for standing up for my feelings and my safety, and what did it get me?

It got me a broken heart; that's what it got me.

I hate thinking of it that way, to the point where it makes me sick to my stomach, but it's the truth. He broke my heart. I trusted him, and he destroyed that. And I don't know who I'm angrier with, him or me. Because I should've known better.

Note to self: don't ever get into a situation like this again. Never, ever can I leave my fate in anybody else's hands. There was no way I could've imagined the night when Alexei found me that things would've ended up this way. There are bad people in the world, people willing to use others so long as it benefits them. They'll say anything to get their way.

Strings are always attached, and there isn't always a way to know what those strings will be. I could never in a million years have guessed who Alexei worked for, for instance, or how I would be expected to pay my debt.

I'll never put myself in that place again. If there's anything I can thank Lucian for, it's that. He taught me a valuable lesson.

He taught me something else, too, something I'm wrestling with even a week later. I need more people in my life, good people, genuine people because I have nobody to turn to right now, and it's enough to make me want him back.

How sick is that? What does that say about me? That I almost wish I could look forward to seeing him again? This whole week, I've bounced back and forth between hating him and missing him. It doesn't make any sense. What's there to miss? When we're together, we're usually doing only one thing. The longest conversation I ever had with him was held in the library when I gave him a safe word that he chose to ignore. I should hate him. I should wish nothing but the worst for him.

But then I remember him coming in and saving me from the psycho with the knife. Talking me through a panic attack. Holding me in his arms until I finally calmed down. It's like he's two different people. It's a shame there's never any telling which version you're going to get from one minute to the next.

It's like I keep attracting men like that into my life. Eric was like that too. He could be charming and funny, even genuinely sweet sometimes. I guess even monsters know how to hide that side of themselves when they need to.

I'm grateful for the knock on the door, and not just because I'm starving. At least eating a pizza gives me something to do besides dwelling on the same stuff I've been obsessing over for a week. I grab my wallet before going to the door, opening it before thinking twice.

And that's a mistake. The door swings open hard enough to bounce off the wall next to it, and I barely have time to get out of the way before Lucian barges into the apartment.

It feels like my heart is going to explode right out of my chest. I run for the kitchen, flailing around, trying to find a weapon. There's a knife in the drawer next to the sink, and I grab it, holding it up at shoulder height. "Stay away from me!"

"Is this really necessary?" He sounds tired, not afraid. Of course, why would he be afraid of somebody like me? I'm nobody, aren't I?

"Is it necessary that you had to practically break into my apartment? What do you think you're doing? You don't belong here. Didn't I make myself clear? Do I need to remind you?" I grip the knife tighter, watching his every move. I can't shake the feeling of waiting for him to strike.

"Put down the knife, Rowan." He begins unbuttoning his suit jacket because, of course, he has to wear a suit everywhere. "I only came to talk."

"That doesn't mean I have to listen. Do you ever get tired of shoving yourself into somebody's life? I didn't ask you to come here, and I have nothing to say to you."

"There are still a few things I want to say."

"You could've called me. Alexei has my number."

"Some things a person doesn't want to say over the phone. Some messages deserve to be delivered face-to-face." I can't believe he's actually making himself comfortable as though he's planning on staying. He takes off his jacket and everything, draping it over one arm before loosening his tie. "It's been a long day."

"I don't care." Still, I can't help but snicker. "What, did you have to sit behind a desk and collect money for work other people are doing? It must be exhausting."

He smirks. "You just described the life of every CEO alive. But I didn't come here for this. I came here to tell you I realize I went too far, and I apologize for that. It was uncalled for and unforgivable. You're absolutely right to take this attitude with me."

I can't help but feel like I'm waiting for the other shoe to drop as we face off from across my tiny kitchen. Does he mean it? Do I want him to? The answer to that is a very pathetic yes. I do. I want him to be telling the truth, and I want to believe him. When am I ever going to stop being weak for men like him?

When he doesn't say anything else for a while, I shrug. "Is that it? Is that what you came to say?"

"I suppose—no, come to think of it, that's not all I came here for."

I should've known. "What else do you want? And don't even consider asking me to put myself through that bullshit again because I won't. So just forget about it."

"That's not it, either. You have to stop jumping to conclusions."

"And maybe you need to stop being so cryptic all the time." When his eyes go wide, I roll mine. "I do know words. I'm not a complete idiot."

"No one ever said you were. I'm just not accustomed to being called out the way you're doing now."

"Yeah, well, if you're looking for an apology, you've come to the wrong place."

"I'm not looking for an apology." His smile even seems genuine. "I was hoping for a little company, to be honest."

All I can do is blink at him. "You're serious."

"I am."

"So you came here. To me. Of all the people in your world."

"What can I say? I enjoy spending time with you."

I don't know if I can believe that or not. What's so special about me? "I'm not having sex with you tonight—or anybody else," I think to add when I remember all the little loopholes people like him use to trick others.

"I wouldn't dream of it." He nods toward the door. "Who did you think I was?"

"The pizza delivery guy."

"I can't tell you the last time I ate fresh pizza. I'm serious," he insists when I shoot him a look. "Do I strike you as someone who has the local joint on speed dial?"

He has a point. And I get the feeling he's inviting himself to share the pizza with me. Well, it's too big for me to eat on my own, anyway.

There's a knock on the door. We exchange a look. "I'll get it for you. Just in case it's another man looking to force his way in." I'm glad he thinks this is hilarious. It's my damn life he's joking around about.

I should put the knife away, shouldn't I? He hasn't made a move beyond taking off his jacket. He hasn't tried to touch me even once. And he did sound sincere when he apologized.

Why am I doing this? I don't know, but I am. The knife goes in the drawer, and I grab napkins before joining Lucian on the sofa, where he's opened the pizza box in the middle of the coffee table. "This smells incredible." He sighs.

"Do you never eat pizza?"

"I tend to stick to healthier foods. But Greta still manages to keep it interesting for me." Yes, I bet she would. I've missed her. "But every so often, I get a craving for extra cheese. It has to be the right kind of pizza, though. That's the tricky part."

"What's the right kind of pizza?"

"Thin crust, but thick enough to have a little bit of bite to it. Puffy at the top, with those little heat blisters." He points at a handful around the edge of our pizza. "This looks like a good one."

"I've never had any complaints." I take a slice and dab away some of the grease before taking a bite. Lucian, meanwhile, peels away a slice, folds it in half, and shoves almost half of it in his mouth all at once.

His eyes close. "Oh, my god. Bliss." So kinky sex isn't the only thing that makes him do that. Here I was, wondering what made him tick. It was pizza all along.

"Sometimes it's good to let yourself go a little, huh?"

"No kidding. Fuck. I have half a mind to buy this place so I can have them deliver to me every day." I bet he could do that, too. Though I keep that thought to myself.

This is too weird. Watching him act like a normal person, asking if there are any movies I'd like to see. He finds a random superhero movie, and I agree since it's not like I'll be paying much attention, anyway. We could watch the Weather Channel for all I care.

How am I supposed to pay attention to anything besides him sitting on the other side of the sofa? All I can do is wonder why he's here and what he wants. Is he going to want to make a thing out of this? I don't know how I feel about that. Sure, it's good to have him with me, but that doesn't mean this will be our new arrangement. His weekly pizza fix or something.

He glances my way after a few minutes. "Why don't you come over here?"

See, I knew it. There had to be something else. "I don't want to. I'm still not over what happened, and I told you that night that I don't want you to touch me again."

His eyes narrow for a second. "I only want to hold you. Nothing sexual." When I scowl, he scowls back. "I think we both know I'd have taken you by now if that's what I came for."

I hate that he's right. If he decided he wanted me, he'd get me. Even if I didn't want him to.

I must be taking too much time making up my mind because his arm darts out and hooks around my waist before I can do anything about it. He doesn't pull me to him, though, not exactly. I end up lying across his lap, facing the TV. "Did that hurt?" he asks. I choose not to answer.

No, it didn't hurt. In fact, this isn't bad at all. Now I know for sure I missed him. His nearness, the way he makes me feel safe—which doesn't really make sense because he's made me feel the exact opposite, too. Maybe he learned his lesson.

Either way, when he reaches out to stroke my hair, I don't flinch away. I'm still not paying attention to the movie, but now it's because his touch is so soothing. The scent of his cologne is nice, too. Years from now, I'll smell that cologne somewhere, and I'll think of him.

Nothing about his touch is demanding. It's gentle, light, and the steady rhythm lulls me into deep relaxation. I haven't exactly been sleeping well—no big surprise.

Nope. My eyes open wide. I'm not going to leave myself vulnerable to him.

But I'm so sleepy.

He wouldn't hurt me. I can fall asleep, and he won't hurt me. I have to believe that because my eyelids are suddenly too heavy to lift any longer.

22

Lucian

It's like I've been granted a precious gift. Her trust, even if it's tentative. Even if she's not sure whether I deserve it. Something deep inside her, some wisdom, tells her what I already know to be true. That I wouldn't hurt her for anything in the world. That she's nothing but safe when we're together.

Now that I know what it's like to be without her, I won't be making any more mistakes.

She's peaceful now, her breathing slow and even. I can't resist the desire to reach down and stroke her hair—gently, barely making contact for fear of waking her and ruining the moment. I've waited a week for this. No, I've waited my entire life for this. So I won't fuck it up now.

Rowan. My precious Rowan. I don't know how many more nights we'll have to go through this little dance. Getting her to trust me, easing her into being close to me. Earning her one inch at a time. I'll do whatever it takes.

It might be because I'm watching her, or it might be because I'm exhausted myself. This hasn't exactly been a restful week. No matter the reason, my head feels heavier with each second until I let it fall back against the sofa cushions.

Which is when I hear the scratching.

I sit up, watchful, listening hard. It isn't loud enough for Rowan to hear—she's still asleep—but it's not mice. That much I know. I can see the door from where we're sitting, and I know it isn't my imagination. The knob is moving ever so slightly like someone is trying to pick the lock and jiggling it as they do.

"Rowan." I shake her gently, lifting her until she's sitting up. She blinks hard, her head lolling a little. "You have to wake up."

"What's wrong?" I hold a finger to my lips before pulling her off the sofa and hurrying her across the room, then into her bedroom.

"Stay in here. Do you hear me? Don't make a sound, and don't come out until I say it's okay." I push her toward the closet and wait until she's inside before creeping out of the room, back toward the front door.

I should let the bastard break in, whoever he is. Let him hear the screeching of the alarm, so he knows what a mistake he made. But no, the alarm isn't set.

That's fine. Whoever it is, I'd like to deal with them one-on-one without police presence.

The lock clicks. I wait, tensed, prepared to end the miserable son of a bitch. When the door opens and reveals who's on the other side, I understand just how miserable he is.

I should've had them kill him when he threw a fit in my club.

Glen's bent at the waist, looking in all directions as he creeps into the apartment. He closes the door behind him, then tiptoes into the living room while I watch from the shadows outside Rowan's bedroom. There's a telltale bulge in his back pocket. The folding blade he's carrying.

Bile rises in my throat when I understand the sort of damage he planned to do to her tonight. I doubt he would've left her alive. When desire is thwarted, it becomes perversion.

When perversion is thwarted, it becomes deadly.

"Who are you looking for, Glen?"

He whirls around, mouth hanging open at the sound of my voice. "You? What are you doing here?"

"I was going to ask you the same question." I step out of the shadows, then away from the bedroom. I want to keep him away from her. "You have no business here."

"You don't know that."

"So, what? You have to break in? Is that part of the fun?" It sickens me since I've done something similar. Only I had no intention of harming her. I wasn't trying to cut her up to make myself feel better.

He's sweating already, eyes darting back and forth. "I only wanted to—"

"To what?" My voice cracks through the air like a whip. "I know what you wanted to do. We both know. Spare me the bullshit." Suddenly, I look toward the door, and he does the same, turning his attention away from me.

And that's when I strike.

I throw myself at him, and we both tumble to the floor between the living room and kitchen. His head hits the hard linoleum floor, and he grunts. I use the opportunity to straddle his chest, pinning his arms to the floor with my knees.

"What? You don't like it when somebody else is in control?" I slam my fist against his face, relishing the blood that oozes from the split flesh over his cheekbone. "You're not much of a man without your knives, are you?" Another blow, then another.

"Pl-please—" It's all he can manage to say before I hit him again. Again. Every time my fist makes contact, a rush of pleasure runs through me. I can't stop myself, and I don't want to. Soon, he's unconscious, limp underneath me.

But I can't stop. I hit him until his face is nothing but jelly. Until nothing about him looks remotely human. By the time I get tired and stop, I'm breathing heavily, but he isn't breathing at all. There's blood all over the kitchen, all over me.

I've never felt like this. Victorious. A lion defending his mate. Before getting up, I spit on him—sick bastard. I don't know how he found out where she lives; he might've followed her home that night when I first took her away from him. Now I'm glad I didn't have him killed. I had the pleasure of doing it myself.

I wash my hands in the sink before calling Alexei. "There's a mess at Rowan's that needs cleaning." With that, I go to her room, then open the closet door.

She's sitting in the corner with her knees against her chest, hands over her ears, eyes closed. It's enough to break my heart. I'll make sure she's never in this position again. "Rowan? Everything's fine now. You're safe."

She scrambles to her feet and throws her arms around me despite the blood on my shirt. "What happened? Are you hurt?"

"It's not my blood." She stiffens in my arms but doesn't pull away.

"Whose is it? Who's out there?"

"It doesn't matter now. Come on. I'm going to take you home." She lifts her head, eyes searching mine. "My home. Where you'll be safe. Close your eyes, and I'll get you out of here." She buries her head in my chest and lets me lead her out of the room, then out of the apartment. I manage to spare her the sight of the corpse in her kitchen.

We wait in the car until Alexei arrives. I didn't want to leave without knowing he got there. I have a short exchange with him, describing what he'll find inside, and from there, I know he can handle things with no further instruction. Nothing matters as much as getting her away from here, keeping her from all of this.

"I can't believe it. If you hadn't been there..." She's shaking, holding on to my arm as I drive. "I don't know what I would've done without you."

"Don't think about it. You're safe now. Nobody will ever hurt you as long as I'm around."

"You killed him." It isn't a question.

She deserves the truth. "I killed him."

Her silence leaves me wondering how she feels, but I won't push her on it. She might need time to process. Not much time, as it turns out. "I was so scared back there. Terrified. Not just for me, either. I was afraid for you."

"You never have to worry about me. I can handle myself."

"Still. I was. I wanted to go out there and help you. I thought, what will I do if anything happens to Lucian? Especially knowing you were defending me. I wouldn't want to live with myself if you didn't make it out of that."

"But I did, Rowan." When it doesn't seem like that makes her feel better, I pull the car over and turn to her, pulling her close. "I'm okay. So are you. There's nothing to be afraid of now."

"There's everything to be afraid of!" She bursts into violent sobs that shake her entire body. "I don't feel safe anywhere. Only when I'm with you. I should be afraid of you after what you did, but all I want is to be with you always because I'm safe with you. I don't know what to think anymore."

I pull her away from my chest and take her face in my hands. Hands I used only minutes ago to kill for her. "Listen to me. If you want, you don't ever have to be afraid again. It doesn't have to be the way it was before. It can be you and me. No arrangements, no encounters. And I swear, I'll do my best to be a better man for you."

Her sobs have quieted into sniffles. "Really?" she whispers, and the hope in it both thrills and humbles me. The most precious, valuable thing in the world, and all she wants is to know I mean what I say.

"Really. I'll do whatever it takes, so long as you're willing to give me another chance."

Her head bobs up and down. "I want that." Anything else she might've wanted to say is muffled when I cover her mouth with mine, taking the kiss I've craved over the endless days we've been apart. She'll never know what a gift she just gave me.

I plan to show her, though—every single day from now on.

EPILOGUE

Rowan

One Year Later

It's dark out here. Quiet as a graveyard. Only I'm not in a graveyard. I'm in the park, and it's the middle of the night. I'm walking fast, hands in my pockets, eyes scanning the area. Pretty, old-fashioned lights dot both sides of the path I'm walking down, but between them, the shadows are as dark as ink. There could be anybody hiding in shadows that deep.

I'm counting on it.

My heels click against the concrete, and the sound echoes all around me. It's chilly, and my breath forms a cloud around my head. I come to a bend in the path and take it, glancing over my shoulder when leaves blow across the ground behind me.

A hand clamps over my mouth before I have the chance to scream, and an arm wraps around my waist. Before I can acknowledge what is happening, I'm being dragged off the path and across the grass. I kick and swing my arms, but it's no use. I can't get him off me.

He throws me against a tree and presses himself against me, pinning me against the trunk. His breath is hot in my face, and his hands are everywhere, running up my skirt, tearing open my blouse. "What's a little girl like you doing walking around the park at this time of night, huh? Wearing these fuck me heels and a skirt so short the whole world can see your ass."

His mouth skims my throat, teeth nipping my earlobe before he whispers in my ear again. "Like you don't want this. Teasing everybody who sees you. Practically begging to get fucked like this."

"Please, don't do this!" I shove at him, slapping his hands frantically when he starts pulling down my thong. "Don't! Stop!"

"Don't stop?" Lucian laughs nastily as he pulls the thong to my ankles, then forces my legs apart with his knee. "Don't worry. I won't."

I fight a little more just for the sake of playing along, but the truth is, I'm soaking wet by the time he shoves his dick into me. He fucks me hard, fast, almost brutally. The way he needs it. The way I like it.

He grunts against my neck. "Fucking slut. Begging to be grabbed. Begging to be fucked hard like this. Showing off those tits." He buries his face in them, and I have to bite back a moan when he finds my nipple and bites down.

"You like that, huh? You like getting fucked like this?"

"Yes... yes..." I close my eyes and give in, not playing anymore. "Fuck me harder."

"Come on this cock, baby. Come for me." He drives himself faster, harder, and we come together in a breathless rush that almost knocks me off my feet. I shudder in his arms, moaning against his shoulder to keep our little secret quiet.

"Oh... Rowan..." He kisses my neck before looking me in the eye. "That was good."

"That was very good." I kiss him before bending down to pull up my underwear. "I'm dressed okay?"

"Are you kidding? I might've settled for watching you and jerking off. Maybe next time, that's all I'll do." There's a wicked little gleam in his eye. He likes to keep me guessing.

He takes my face in his hands, smiling. Now he's just Lucian. Not the powerful business owner. Not the man with connections to just about all kinds of shady, scary people. I can't even remember why I was so afraid of him at one time. "You're incredible. Thank you for being so perfect for me."

"Hey. It's not like I don't get anything out of it." But that's not completely honest. It doesn't say anything about what's going on in my heart. And all of a sudden, saying what's in my heart seems very important. Why it should seem so crucial after a year of being together, I don't know. The moment just feels right.

"I love you."

His eyes widen a little. For a second, I'm afraid I said the wrong thing. I should've kept it to myself. This is why I need to keep my mouth shut instead of randomly spouting things off. It must be the whole coming-off-an-orgasm thing. "I'm sorry. I shouldn't have—"

"I love you, too." He strokes my cheeks with his thumbs. "Did you think you had to apologize? You took me off guard, is all. But the feeling's there, Rowan. It's always been there."

I'm so relieved, I could cry. "Thank you." Now I can't help but laugh. "I'm all mixed up."

"You're perfect just the way you are." He kisses me softly before touching his forehead to mine. He's come such a long way this year. My protector, yes, but also my love. Being indebted to him was the best thing that could've happened to both of us.

He pulls me along with him, headed for where he left the car. "Come on. Let's go home so I can give you a bath and a back rub. You've earned both."

The man makes a good argument.

∼

Thank You for reading Hell, book two in the Heaven & Hell series. If you enjoyed this book don't forget to check out book three in this series Hitman.

HEAVEN & HELL
WHERE EVEN YOUR KINKIEST DREAMS COME TRUE

Bleeding Heart Press presents Heaven & Hell, a taboo romance series by ten of your favorite best-selling authors.
Welcome to Purgatory, an exclusive club where we transform your darkest desires into reality. Here, everything is possible and nothing is too taboo.
Test your limits and find the kink you never knew you needed.
Newsletter Signup

Books in this Series:
Heaven by Darcy Rose
Hell by J.L. Beck and C. Hallman
Hitman by Isabella Starling and C. Hallman
Poisoned Paradise by Lucy Smoke
Possessive by Vivan Wood
Wrong by Adelaide Forrest
Decent by Sam Mariano
More to come...

ALSO BY THE AUTHORS

<u>CONTEMPORAY ROMANCE</u>

North Woods University
The Bet
The Dare
The Secret
The Vow
The Promise
The Jock

Bayshore Rivals
When Rivals Fall
When Rivals Lose
When Rivals Love

Breaking the Rules
Kissing & Telling
Babies & Promises
Roommates & Thieves

Also by the Authors

***

DARK ROMANCE

The Blackthorn Elite
Hating You
Breaking You
Hurting You
Regretting You

The Obsession Duet
Cruel Obsession
Deadly Obsession

The Rossi Crime Family
Protect Me
Keep Me
Guard Me
Tame Me
Remember Me

The Moretti Crime Family
Savage Beginnings
Violent Beginnings
Broken Beginnings

The King Crime Family
Indebted
Inevitable

Diabolo Crime Family
Devil You Hate
Devil You Know

ABOUT THE AUTHORS

J.L. Beck and **C. Hallman** are *USA Today* and international bestselling author duo who write contemporary and dark romance.

Find us on facebook and check out our website for sales and freebies!

www.bleedingheartromance.com

Printed in Great Britain
by Amazon